Trapped
by the Tide

and other stories

By the same author

THE GREY APPLE TREE

CARRY A LONG KNIFE

SHIPWRECK

Trapped by the Tide

and other stories

VERA CUMBERLEGE

Illustrated by Gavin Rowe

ANDRE DEUTSCH

For Jenny and Oliver

First published 1977 by
André Deutsch Limited
105 Great Russell Street London WC1

Printed in Great Britain by
Cox and Wyman Ltd
London, Fakenham and Reading

ISBN 0 233 96899 7

Contents

Trapped
by the Tide

Bob was digging for sand eels along the edge of the sea. The tide was out and a mile of sand stretched between him and the shore. The day had been sunny and warm but now a mist was slowly thickening and the sun was as pale as the moon. Bob grabbed at the slippery fish bait as he dumped each spadeful of sand by the side of the hole, then put the sand eels in a bucket, where they squirmed over each other.

The tide had turned and was running between the ridges of sand, spilling into the hole he had dug, flattening the piles of sand, moving steadily towards the distant shore now barely visible in the mist. He picked up the bucket, swung the big spade on to his shoulder and started for home.

He stopped suddenly for someone somewhere had laughed loudly. He looked all round. There were no children digging sand castles. The summer visitors had all gone. The school holidays were over and the village shops had put away their picture postcards and shrimping nets. He had seen no one, but in the thickening mist someone might have come by. Perhaps it was the sunny October day that had brought visitors to the village. 'They must be in a boat,' he thought and looked seaward where the pale sun broke the ripples into a thousand points of light. He screwed up his eyes. The buoy that marked the harbour entrance was only visible because he knew where to look for it. There was no boat to be seen. Then he saw that there was someone on the sand bar.

The sand bar was a long bank of sand, uncovered only at low tide, a favourite place for collectors of fine shells, but

9

where the tide must be watched, for once it had turned, the
sea quickly filled the channel on the landward side before
spreading over the sand to the shore. During the summer
one of the coastguards would train a telescope on the bar
and if anyone lingered the 'woop woop' of the siren would
send its warning across the sands.

But who would walk the mile to the sand bar on an
afternoon grown misty, in the middle of October? Their
boat must be hidden on the far side of the bar. Bob hesitated. The sand moved under his bare feet as the sea
trickled beneath them. He would have to wade out against

the incoming tide if he wanted to make sure, and that
would make him late home and his father needed the fish
bait; but he quickly made up his mind and started through
the shallow water. He must make sure there was a boat or
it would soon be too late to wade across the channel which
must already be full of water. He looked back towards the
land, but it was only a faint blur. Even if the coastguards
were on the look out they could not see far on a day like
this.

   He put down his bucket and, propping his spade against
his leg, cupped his hands and shouted, 'Ahoy there!'

Now he could see there were two figures on the bar. 'Come on,' he shouted. 'Hurry!'

They had been kneeling and now they stood up. Bob splashed towards them, hitching his rolled-up trousers higher, knowing as he did so that it was a waste of time for the water was already knee high. Now he could see them clearly, a tall girl and a shorter one. As he neared them he saw there was also a boy still kneeling on the sand.

Again he shouted, 'Have you a boat?' They only stared. 'A boat. Have you a boat?'

'No,' the bigger girl called back.

As he took the next step Bob felt his feet slipping. He had reached the edge of the channel. He heaved his bucket on to his shoulder, pushed his toes into the sand and with the spade to balance him he waded through the water which came above his waist in the deepest part.

As he walked up on to firm sand the younger girl burst out laughing. 'Look Alice, he was swimming with his clothes on!'

'Don't be rude, Dolly, and don't speak to him. Mum said we mustn't speak to strangers.' She turned her back.

Bob stood on the highest part of the sand bar, still a couple of feet above the water. There was no boat on the far side. 'Is your dad coming for you?' he asked, hoping he might be fishing somewhere near.

'What's that got to do with you?' Alice, the taller girl asked in reply, and without waiting for an answer went on, 'As it happens he is helping Mum unpack.'

'Then you don't know it's dangerous out here. Come on, it's getting deeper every minute.'

'I'm not going your way,' Dolly, the younger one announced. 'I'm going back the way we came where it's dry,' and she ran off along the top of the bar, her fair hair in its careful ringlets bouncing on her shoulders.

Bob turned to Alice. 'Tell her to come back or you'll all be drowned.'

Alice faced him, expecting him to laugh and say he had only spoken in fun. He was not looking at her, and she studied his serious face for a moment before following the direction of his eyes. Except for the sand bank there was no land to be seen, only mist and sea.

It was the first time her family had come to this seaside village. They had been told there were miles of sand, and the three of them had run down to the beach while their parents unpacked. They had chased each other over the sand and had paddled in shallow pools, always looking for the sea which they knew must be there somewhere. Several times Alice thought they should turn back, but her small brother Edward was enjoying it all so much that she had gone on till they had climbed a sand bank and found the sea on the other side. They were collecting shells till this boy came out of the mist to tell them they would drown.

'It was all sand just now,' she said.

'The tide comes in very fast, that's why it's dangerous.'

'Oh,' was all Alice could think of saying. She didn't understand how it had happened so quickly, but Bob didn't look the kind of boy who would joke about drowning, though he carried a bucket and spade. She only thought of sand castles for Edward, and the boy looked too old to be making castles. There was no time to ask him, for Dolly came running up.

'It's all water –' she began, and without warning opened her mouth wide and howled, 'Mum! Mum! I want Mum!' Then she began to cry; not quiet crying but in furious yells. As the tears ran down her face she rushed at Bob and beat him with her fists. 'You beastly boy!' she screamed.

Bob looked at Alice in bewilderment as the bigger girl dragged Dolly away. 'Sorry,' she panted, 'she gets upset. It's because of Edward.' She nodded towards the small boy who had his shells spread in a pattern on the sand. He had not moved but was watching them with frightened eyes.

Bob rubbed his bruised arm. 'You had better take her, and pick her up if it gets too deep. I'll carry Edward.' He held out his hand. The little boy backed away.

'He won't go with you. He's deaf and that makes him shy.'

'You mustn't tell!' Dolly shrieked. 'You mustn't tell on Edward. It's not fair. It's not his fault.'

'Of course it's not his fault.' Bob spoke indignantly. 'But you're frightening him. Do come on or we'll have to swim, and I don't expect you can swim.'

Dolly was calm enough to say, 'Anyway, I won't swim in my clothes. Mum said we mustn't get wet.'

'Then take them off and hold them over your head and I'll carry you through the deepest part.'

'I won't let you carry me. Go away.'

Bob looked at Alice. 'You go on with Edward,' he said. He thought that Dolly would come with him if Alice went ahead; but it was not like that. Edward didn't want to leave his shells and he fought Alice as she picked him up. She struggled with him down the slope to the water's edge, and then Dolly rushed at her. Before Bob could catch her she had helped Edward to break free, and he had scrambled up the bank in soundless panic.

Dolly threw herself down and wound her arms round him crying, 'I love my brother. You mustn't touch him.'

That did nothing to calm the little boy who could not hear or understand, and he was still more frightened when she kicked and yelled as Bob tried to pick her up. Alice tried again to lift Edward, but in the end they had to give up, and they stood back defeated.

'You'll have to go for help,' Bob told Alice.

'I can't,' she answered. 'I promised to look after them. You go.'

One part of Bob's mind said 'Why not? It's their fault.' Another part of his mind said, 'You will always remember, all your life long. Like old Dan who tells how he swam away and left a man with a rope caught round his foot; he was drowned before help came, and Dan goes on telling the story year after year.' Aloud he said, 'Listen, Alice, there's no time to explain, just do as I say. You see that dark sort of line?' he pointed towards the shore. 'It's not very clear, so don't take your eyes off it. Get there, and tell anyone you meet that we're on the sand bar and they'll send a boat,' he pushed her.

'No,' she protested, 'I can't go.'

'You're afraid like Dolly, I suppose?'

'It's not that.'

'Afraid of getting your dress wet?'

'No.'

'Then go. You can save us.'

'I can't swim.'

'It won't be over your head.'

'I must take them with me.' Hearing her, Dolly dragged Edward farther away.

Bob pushed Alice till she was waist deep. 'Careful,' he said, 'it will only be really deep at the bottom of the channel.'

Alice tried to turn back, but loose sand carried her down and she had to take another step forward.

At a wail from Dolly Bob waded back. He held out his hand to her. For a moment he thought she would come. Instead she clutched Edward and shouted to Alice to come back.

The water in the channel was up to her chin, and Alice found it hard to keep her balance. She dared not look round, yet she hated going on. 'I can't leave them,' she kept saying to herself. 'I can't tell Mum and Dad I've left them.' She stumbled, and only by splashing wildly with her arms did she stop herself from falling. Another step and the water was round her waist. She turned.

'Run!' Bob called.

Dolly and Edward were clinging together, 'Even if I go

back,' she thought, 'they won't come.' She felt the tide pushing her towards the shore, yet it was hard to move fast, and she seemed to get no nearer the shore. 'I must get there. I must get there,' she said over and over again.

On the sand bar Bob watched Alice's shadowy figure disappear in the mist. She ought to reach the land safely but – he stopped himself. It was no use thinking how long it would take her to get there. He turned round. Deaf Edward had broken away from Dolly and, still not under-standing what the fuss was about, had gone back to his shells and was placing them in a careful pattern.

The few deaf people Bob knew were old and seemed stupid, answering questions no one had asked and getting things wrong however loudly one shouted down their ear trumpets. Perhaps like this boy they had clever ideas. He would give his grandmother a pencil and paper next time he saw her. Next time – a wave broke lightly against the sand bar, ran over the top and down the other side, cutting a channel through the careful pattern. Edward sprang back. Another wave followed and he jumped up and ran across the few paces of dry sand straight into the sea. Bob was after him at once but could not catch him before he had fallen on his face. Dolly screamed as Bob carried the dripping boy back to safety. She started to speak but Bob cut her short, saying angrily, 'Be quiet, you stupid girl.'

He wished he had not spoken as he was sure she would cry again and he was afraid he might hit her. Instead of crying, he saw a blush spreading over her face and she turned her back. Dolly, the pretty one, spoilt by her father, made much of and admired, heard an unknown boy call her stupid and knew it was true.

The sand round her heels felt alive as the last dry patches disappeared, then there was only sea and mist and herself in the middle, and the strange boy pulling his jersey over his head and wrapping it round her shivering brother. With sudden anger at herself she knew that she had only been showing off when she screamed and refused to go with Alice. Showing off to this boy. She hadn't protected Edward, poor frightened Edward who would have gone with Alice if she had helped. She had wanted the boy to see that her brother loved her better than Alice and would do what she said. Her thoughts were not very clear, more a jumble of anger and fear, for in the moving, sliding sand there seemed to be hands with long fingers closing round her feet, trying to pull her under.

'Are we going to drown?' she asked.

Bob pushed his spade into the shifting sand, then turned his bucket upside down letting the sand eels wriggle away and vanish. He stood Edward on the bucket, keeping an arm round him. Only when he had him safely in place did he answer, and then his reply was an abrupt, 'I don't know.'

When she said nothing he looked at her and now noticed that she was very pretty though her fair ringlets clung damply round her face, and her large blue eyes were afraid. He remembered a drowned seaman he had seen carried ashore from a wreck. For a man to fight the sea in the fury of a storm and lose the battle was one thing, but not for Dolly to stand on the sand bar on a calm day till the tide lifted her curls and gently carried her away; that must not happen if he could help it.

'Come and hold on to the spade,' he said, 'and we'll make a plan.'

Cautiously Dolly took a step towards him. He couldn't help her for fear of Edward falling, but as she reached him and put her hand on the spade he covered it with his own and held her firmly.

'We've still a little time.' He spoke carefully for the sea was creeping up his legs and he had to fight the desire to swim away to the now hidden shore. 'First let's shout in case Alice has got a boat.'

'Already?' Dolly asked. 'It took us ages to get here.'

'Perhaps it's too soon, but you never know. We'll turn a bit so we face out to sea. Come on. One – two – three – help!' they both shouted.

The mist seemed to draw itself closer round them. Edward could not hear their shout but he felt the movement and struggled in the folds of Bob's jersey. Bob looked down and smiled and the little boy stood quietly once more on the unsteady bucket.

'We'll call again,' Bob said.

'But it's no use. You're only pretending.' Dolly's voice shook.

'I'm not pretending. Don't you see it's the same for me, and a boat might come by; but let's make a plan in case no boat comes. When the water is as high as your chin it'll be up to your brother's chin too; then I'll tie the arms of my jersey round my neck with Edward inside it and I'll swim on my back. You must hold on to him and kick with your legs.'

He could feel her trembling. 'We'll be under water if you swim.'

'No you won't. Not if you keep your head up, but you must kick your legs and keep them right out of my way.'

'I don't know how,' Dolly wailed.

'Then shout.' Panic was rising in him, though he fought to keep calm. He could never swim with both of them, and shouting for help only increased his fear. Suddenly Dolly gave a lurch as the tide lifted her off her feet. She clutched at Bob who tried to catch her. For an instant he loosened his grasp on Edward who fought his way out of the thick fisherman's jersey. The bucket turned over and as Bob caught him, the small boy flung his arms round Bob's neck in a strangling hold. The jersey floated slowly away.

Bob staggered about trying to regain his foothold. He caught the spade handle and steadied himself; then grabbed a handful of curls and pulled Dolly's head above water. She seized his arm, coughing and spluttering, turning her blue eyes up to his face in shocked surprise as if it was he who had pushed her under. The plans he had tried to make were useless. He could not swim at all with arms so tight round his neck.

'Help!' he shouted, though his voice sounded dead in the thickening mist. He tried to lift Dolly's head higher, but now she made no effort to help herself and he couldn't do much with the weight of Edward pulling him down and the water up to his chin.

'Keep your head up, Dolly,' he begged, 'I can't hold you.' He felt her slipping. 'Oh help, help!'

Through the mist a voice answered, 'Ahoy there!'

'Here! Quick!'

The voice a little fainter this time. 'I can't find you.'

'Here! This way!'

Dolly screamed, 'Don't go away!' She tried to run towards the voice and disappeared under water. Bob was dragged after her.

The stranglehold round his neck tightened. He lost his grip on the spade. His head went under as he slipped off the top of the sand bar. He kicked wildly trying to find the spade again but he only thickened the water with whirling sand. Suddenly the strangling arms loosened and he threw up his head gasping for breath, one hand clutching at the thin legs that were swept from his grasp. In horror at losing the little boy he reached up at the vanishing legs and saw a man above him leaning from a boat, with Edward in his arms.

Bob found he still had a handful of Dolly's hair. She was beating the water with her hands and though she swallowed a lot, she was keeping herself afloat. He pulled her close to the boat and the man lifted her in.

A great cheerfulness seized Bob which made him shout, 'Wait a minute.' He duck-dived and swam in a circle looking for the spade. It was new, and his father would not be pleased if he lost it. He saw it lying, already partly covered with sand. Picking it up by the handle he kicked upward. Though he was only a few feet under water, the weight of the spade and his sodden trousers slowed his rise and before he broke the surface, water rushed down his throat. He struggled and coughed as water and air mixed. He could no longer think, but rose and sank, clutching the spade and thrashing the water with his other hand. Then his shirt was seized and his head stayed in the air.

'Got another child there?' The voice seemed to roar in his ears. Bob lifted the spade which seemed such a heavy weight. The man leant over the stern of the small boat and took it. When he saw what it was he nearly dropped it, but changed his mind and put it behind him. Bob heaved himself in. He lay half in half out of the boat while the water ran out of his mouth; then he slid farther in and lay for a moment thinking how wonderful the bottom of a boat looked.

The boatman did what he could for the two children by taking off his oilskin coat and wrapping it round them. By the time Bob had got to his knees the man had the oars out and was already rowing.

'Are they all right?' Bob asked, peering round the boat-man at the children huddled in the bows. How pinched and cold the small boy looked. Bob wished he had some dry clothes to give him. He was glad when Dolly drew him right under the large coat out of the chill fog.

The boatman spoke roughly, 'What did you do that for?'

'It's Father's spade. I've lost his bait and I don't want to lose this too.'

The boatman snorted. 'You know what I meant. Getting cut off like that.'

Before Bob could think of an answer, Dolly called out, Where's Alice?'

'Who's Alice?'

'She went for help,' Bob answered, and thought –

Alice! Had he done wrong in letting her go by herself. Yet what else could he have done? He looked over the side to see how the tide was running. 'If you want to make harbour, it's over there,' he pointed, then added, 'you're a stranger here, aren't you?'

The boatman nodded. 'First time I've been around here. I'm from the yacht *Dancing Lady*. We heard you shout.'

'You want to get back to her?'

'No. The skipper's bringing her in at high tide.'

Bob rubbed his cold hands together as he pictured the graceful lines of the yacht. If the fog lifted he might see her cutting the blue sea, the foam white along her hull, her sails set to catch the breeze. His shirt clung cold and wet. He thought of his jersey and wondered if he would find it one day among the seaweed and driftwood, or if it was caught under a rock where it would lie till it rotted away. How was he going to explain its loss to his mother without upsetting her by saying he had nearly drowned. He wouldn't have to say much to his father, he would understand. If only he could get warm. 'Can I take an oar?' he asked.

'No!' came the sharp reply. Then in a more friendly tone the boatman went on, 'You keep a look-out for me.'

The boatman glanced at Bob now and again, where he sat alert, turning his head quickly to peer through the fog trying to pick up landmarks. He wondered if he had been wrong, for somehow Bob did not seem the sort of boy who would lead children into danger. If he had been rescuing them, why didn't he say so?

They passed a breakwater; then a building loomed through the fog, and Bob called 'Steady.'

The boatman looked over his shoulder and saw a landing-stage ahead of them. As they neared it they heard voices. A man was shouting, 'Hurry! You're not trying! Pull harder!'

Bob recognized the voice that answered as one of the local fishermen who was having his boat repaired in the

boat yard. He shouted back, 'Sorry sir, we can't get her floated for a few minutes yet.'

The local men were trying to pull a motor launch off the harbour mud. Water was already lapping round its sides and soon it would be free and heading out of the harbour against the force of the incoming tide. Though the men strained to get the launch afloat they had no hope of reaching the sand bar in time; but that did not stop them from trying.

The landing-stage seemed to swim towards them through the mist as Dolly poked her head from under the oilskin. 'It's my dad!' she shrieked. 'Dad! Dad!' and she stretched her arms up to a man at the top of the landing-stage.

The fisherman standing at the bottom of the weed-covered steps, dropped the rope he had been pulling, caught hold of the boat and drew in alongside. The childrens' father started down, but the steps were too slippery for his town shoes and he was pulled back before he fell. The boatman stood up and lifted Dolly and passed her to the fisherman. She was so cramped and stiff that he had to carry her up and put her in her father's arms. Little deaf Edward was carried to his mother who had been crying in the background where Alice, soaked and exhausted, had been trying to comfort her.

Bob picked up his spade. He looked at the boatman. 'Thanks,' he said. That didn't seem enough, and he tried to think what more he could say to the man who had saved his life. He gazed into the mist but it gave him no help. The boatman said nothing. So muttering 'Thanks' once again, he ran up the steps.

Before he reached the top the fisherman caught his arm. 'Hey, Bob,' he said, 'what have you been up to?'

Bob grinned, 'Having a swim, beautiful day for swimming!'

The fisherman knew him well and laughed. 'A bit of life-saving as well?' he asked.

'He's the one.' Bob pointed to the boatman. 'Thank him for me.'

He leapt up the last few steps, glancing at the family tangled in each others arms. Alice broke away and came towards him. He gave her a wave and vanished into the mist.

Smuggler's Cave

MARTIN never got to sleep quickly on the first night of a holiday. He lay snugly inside his sleeping bag with his head outside the tent watching the reflections on the darkening sea from the lights of a town far across the bay. Tim was already asleep.

The Cornford family – father, mother, Martin and Tim – had been lent an old coastguard cottage in a field overlooking the sea above a fishing village. They had not come through the village, as there was only a footpath from there to the cottage, but had turned their car off the main road, through a farm gate marked 'Private'. Then they had bumped along a farm road over several fields till they reached another gate also marked 'Private'. Beyond the gate was their own private field. They could scramble down through rough grass to the beach which was almost private too, as it was completely blocked on one side by fallen rocks, and was cut off from the village at high tide by other rocks.

Martin and Tim had brought their tent, and as they put it up they agreed that it was the best camp site they had ever had. They cooked sausages for the family in a brick fireplace behind the tent, and when it grew dark their parents had gone back to the cottage, where they left the back door unlocked in case a storm got up, or it got too cold for sleeping out. But the weather was fine and the night air only cool on Martin's face. The sound of the waves slapping on the shore was soothing, and at last Martin slept.

He must have slept for several hours; then he opened his eyes and, for a moment, wondered where he was; then he

saw the stars and remembered. It was much colder, and he
reached out to let down the tent flap. It was then that he
heard the sound that must have woken him – the sound of a
car being driven on the farm road near their gate, the one
marked 'Private'.

He reached over to Tim's sleeping bag and shook it.
'Tim! Wake up. Listen.' Only a grunt answered him.

Martin crawled out of his sleeping bag and looked towards the gate. He could hear the car quite plainly but the
sound grew fainter as it was driven away along the rough
farm road. It was possible that someone had taken the
wrong turning, though they had shut the gate by the main
road. Even that would not explain the thing that was
puzzling him: the car was being driven without lights.
There was no point now in waking Tim; so Martin pulled
on an extra blanket, shut the tent flap, and did not wake
again till his father shouted to them that breakfast was
ready.

After breakfast Martin told Tim what he had heard.
They walked up the field, climbed over the gate and looked
for tyre marks in the dusty farm road. There were a lot of
marks which told them nothing, except that cars and
tractors had made them.

Tim pointed. 'There's a car. That must be the one you heard.'

Just down the farm road was another gate. It stood open and in the field was a car. A man was walking towards it. Martin and Tim walked down to the gate and stood watching as the man got in and turned the car.

As he reached the gate Martin called out, 'Shall I shut it for you?'

The man leant out of the window. 'You camping over there?' When Martin nodded he added, 'You must be the Cornfords. My wife told me you'd arrived. This is all my land. I hope it stays fine for you.'

'Thank you Mr –' Martin said.

'Stevens is the name.'

As the car began to move Jim asked, 'Can you get down to the shore from this field?' Mr Stevens looked surprised, and Jim went on, 'Martin thought he heard someone up here in the middle of the night.'

The farmer smiled. 'You've been reading stories of smugglers. There used to be a lot of smuggling round here in the olden days. My boys were always hoping that one day they would find the cave, filled with kegs of brandy.'

'Is there a cave?'

The farmer looked at them thoughtfully, wondering whether to give them permission to go through his field and down to the little cove cut off from the rest of the shore by fallen rocks. Would they leave his gate open or drop broken glass that could cut the feet of his cattle? He would chance it. 'You'd like to see the cave?' he asked.

'Yes please, Mr Stevens,' Martin answered.

'Can Mum and Dad come too?' Jim asked.

It was the farmer's turn to look pleased. 'Yes, of course. Do they like caves?'

'It's fossils mostly. If you don't mind us looking for them? Dad can get them out of the cliff without breaking them, and Mum helps us to mount them.'

'Stones too,' Martin put in. 'We collect them every holiday. We found an iron pyrite, like gold. And a piece of amber in Norfolk. I've got a bit of rock crystal.' Martin felt in his pockets and showed the farmer the small lump like a piece of glass.

'That's nice,' he said. 'You must come to the farm and see our collection. Nothing grand, just bits we have picked up on the shore. It's after storms that we find the best things.'

'Any drowned men?' Jim asked gloatingly.

'Even that, once. But I don't recommend it. Fossils are better. Well, I must go. I'll call round later and get you all down for tea.'

'We will keep the gate shut, Mr Stevens,' Martin said.

'And we'll tell everyone its private,' Jim called after him. 'Private, just for us.'

They raced back to the cottage.

The path to the cove was narrow and overgrown. They followed its windings down through thorn trees, then through gorse which they cut back to save their legs, and then through thick grass, and so down to the beach.

While their mother got a picnic ready, the boys and their father explored. It did not take them long as the cove was small; but a bit of cliff looked right for fossils. The cave was among piled rocks, with a narrow entrance like the opening to a tent. It was dark inside, but their father had a torch. They found the cave widened, and even a tall man could stand upright. The ground sloped up and it was plain to see that at high tide half the cave would be flooded, though the far end seemed dry. A deep shelf had been cut in the end wall well above the highest tide mark. Their father examined the shelf.

'This isn't natural,' he said.

Tim scrambled on to it. 'It's where the smugglers used to hide their booty,' he said. 'Mr Stevens told us. Ages ago, of course.'

'Yes, modern smugglers wouldn't use a place like this.'

'You mean they build secret panels in their cars,' Martin said, 'and false bottoms to their suitcases for watches and drugs –'

'They use boats, too,' Tim broke in. 'I've read about it, and if they got chased they might dump their cargo here.'

'Perhaps so. It's exciting to read about the old smugglers but the drug smuggling that goes on today is horrible; making huge sums of money out of human misery.'

It was damp and cold in the cave and they were glad to come out into the sun.

Having their own private cove added to the fun of the holiday, yet there was so much to do and so many places to explore that they did not go there often; though it was from there that they added a fine ammonite fossil to their collection. It was nearly as good as the one Mr Stevens had. He had some unusual things in his collection, including a brass fitting which must have come from a sunken ship, and a silver spoon and a cannon ball.

It was nearly the end of the holiday when Martin again woke very early in the morning before it was light. He put his head out through the tent flap and listened. With all the fun they had been having he had forgotten about their first night; now it all came back to him. There was no moon and the sea was black, for the stars were hidden behind clouds that were driven across the sky by a wind that was rising and making the tent strain at its guy ropes; but it was not the sea or the clouds that interested him, it was the sound of a car.

The car was up by the gate, and Martin was determined that this time he would take a look at it. He thought of waking Tim but knew it would take so long that he decided to leave him. He pulled on his dark blue fisherman's jersey and crept out of the tent and up the field towards the gate. He was only half-way when the noise of the engine grew louder and he made out the dark shape of a car being driven from Mr Stevens' field towards the main road. He crouched down as again he saw that the car showed no lights. As it went slowly away he wondered how the driver managed to keep to the farm road. When it had disappeared he got up and climbed through the fence by the gate, keeping low to avoid being seen.

The summer night would soon be over, but the clouds were thick and dark, a drop of rain splashed in his face. The gate into Mr Stevens' field stood open. Did that mean that the people in the car were coming back, or was some-one still there?

There were no sheep or cattle in the field so there was no reason for Mr Stevens to be there in the dark, and Martin could see no moving shapes; but was someone using the cove, or even the cave?

He went back to the tent and shook Tim. As he expected it took quite a time to get him awake. Then they ate apples while Martin explained what had happened. Tim thought they should get their father to go with them if they were going to the cave in the dark.

'You know he doesn't like being woken in the night,' Martin objected. 'He will just say "Have a glass of milk. That will send you to sleep," like he does if I have a nightmare. Anyhow I'm going down to see if anything's there. It will soon be light and we've got a torch.' As Tim said nothing, he added, 'Don't come if you don't want to.'

Tim pulled on his jersey. He couldn't stay by himself not knowing what had happened, and he knew that Martin wanted him. Of course it was just the cold wind that made him shiver.

They walked silently up the field, clambered through the fence and into Mr Stevens' field. Tim wished it would hurry up and get light, for the bushes and stunted trees looked so like people. Martin did not use his torch in the open; but when they went down the narrow pathway to the shore he shone it on the ground at their feet. He stopped where the path emerged from the trees and whispered, 'If they come back we'll hide over there in the bushes and keep quiet till they've gone.'

Tim wished he knew who 'they' were. He tried to listen for footsteps but could only hear the waves splashing on the rocks and the wind whistling through the trees. 'Let's hide now till it gets lighter,' he begged.

Martin had been thinking the same thing till Tim voiced his fears. That made him feel braver, and he laughed and said, 'Don't be a coward. There isn't anyone coming, and there won't be anything in the cave. There must be a simple reason for the car. It's just fun to make this an adventure.'

He might have believed his own words if it had not been for the open gate and the fact that the car had no lights. They couldn't turn back now they had come so far, and if those in the car were smugglers they might have left a clue in the cave which should be found before the next high tide washed the sand smooth and clean.

It started to rain. Even so it was getting light and they could see the waves as they broke against the rocks. Using the torch once or twice where bushes almost covered the path, they crept down to the beach. Tim wished he had not come. He longed to be back in the tent. He did not want to go into the cave, even to find drugs worth thousands of pounds. Caves are beastly, he thought, even in daylight, even with Dad. Martin never seemed to mind; there he was

34

scrambling over fallen rocks towards the cave expecting him to be close behind.

When Martin reached the entrance to the cave he stopped and waited for Tim to join him. 'We must find things together,' he thought, pushing away the idea that he needed Tim beside him to give him courage to go into that dank cave smelling of rotting seaweed.

'If it's drugs, they will be on the shelf at the back,' Martin whispered to Tim who was now beside him. 'We must look for clues as we go along, I'll shine the torch on the ground . . .'

Tim wanted to ask what sort of clues he was to look for, but he could not stop his teeth from chattering. Perhaps it was fear, though it might have been the cold. It was more like winter than July with the rain, and the wind blowing spray all over him. He followed Martin through the narrow entrance to the cave. At once the noise of the wind and waves was muffled, yet the air was colder than outside – cold and still and dark. He kept close to Martin, trying not to trip over the stones that littered half the cave and which seemed to move about in the wavering light of the torch. There was no clue to be found among the stones.

When they reached the sand Martin stopped and Tim bent down and saw a jumble of footprints. The silence seemed to press him down, making it hard to breathe; he clenched his teeth to keep them quiet as he tried to listen, but he could only hear a bumping noise that was his own heart thumping.

Martin shone his light slowly across the footprints till it came to rest, to his horror, on a bare foot! A dark foot, with toes digging into the sand as the owner could retreat no farther. The silence of the cave was shattered by a loud yell from Tim. He clutched Martin's arm, jerking the torch upward, and a dozen eyes shone in the darkness. Tim turned and rushed back towards the entrance. Forgetting about the stones, he tripped over them and, catching his

head on the rough side of the cave, he lay stunned. For a moment Martin kept his light on the dark faces in front of him, then he swung quickly round and, in the torch light, saw Tim lying on the stones.

A soft voice behind him said, 'My goodness, I think he is hurt,' and a man pushed by him and went and bent over Tim. He was already trying to get up, holding back the sobs of pain that kept rising in his throat.

'It's all right, Tim,' Martin tried to sound calm. 'It's all right, you needn't be afraid.'

'No, do not be afraid,' said the man who was looking first at Tim's bruised head and then at a gash in his knee. 'We are all good men.'

Suddenly Martin realized that he was an Asian, and he shone his torch towards the others. Five more were shivering in thin suits with their shoes hung round their necks. Suitcases were balanced on the shelf behind them.

36

'You can't stay here,' Martin called out. 'Once the tide is in you can't leave without getting soaked, as the rocks will be under water.'

The man at his side spoke. 'They do not understand. Please be so good as to tell me what is this "tide".'

'The sea comes in. Swish!'

How childish that sounded. Martin hoped the man was not offended, but he wasn't sure how else to make him understand. The stranger had turned to his companions and was talking fast. Fear sprang into the dark eyes. Martin kept the beam of his torch on them as they put on their shoes and picked up their cases. He wondered if they were full of drugs.

They crowded round Tim. One of them put his suitcase down and opening it he fumbled among a few clothes and then produced a large clean handkerchief which he insisted on tying round Tim's knee. Two of them helped him up, though he kept protesting that he could walk alone. It was plain he needed help and Martin could see they were friendly. He picked up one case. It was so light that there could be little in it. Only as he started to guide them towards the entrance did it occur to him that it was not drugs that were being smuggled, but men. These dark skinned Asians had been smuggled into England without passports. Someone had rowed them ashore in the dark and left them in the cave like the brandy casks of long ago. He wanted to stop and think what was the right thing to do, but they pressed close to him trying to keep their feet within the circle of light.

As they reached the entrance spray whipped into their faces and several cried out in alarm; but Martin walked ahead into the grey light of a rainy dawn, and they were able to see that though the waves ran among the rocks they could scramble over them to the path. Tim was glad of support for his head hurt and he couldn't bend his knee.

They went slowly up the path, Martin leading the way.

He wondered why they followed him. Perhaps they thought he knew what should be done with them. Looking back, his one thought was to get them under cover and dry. The rain was turning their thin suits black and their shoes were plastered with mud. They stood panting when they reached the top and gazed round at the empty fields.

'The car?' The one who spoke English sounded alarmed. Martin spun round, but there was no car in sight. The man had only asked a question, but it was obvious they were expecting one to take them on the next stage of their journey. Martin suddenly felt afraid. What would the smugglers do when they found their hide-out had been discovered?

'This way,' he said, and went through the open gate. Then he opened the gate marked 'Private' that led into their field. The men straggled after him, Tim hobbling along as fast as he could between two helping hands, afraid of losing sight of Martin.

The coastguard cottage was in darkness. Martin led the way to the back door which was always left unlocked for them. He switched on the light in the kitchen and turned to watch as they came slipping and sliding over the wet grass. There was still no sign of a car as he shut the door on the last of them. Tim lowered himself into a chair, with his cut leg sticking out stiffly in front of him.

Was it safe to leave Tim, Martin wondered. He did not want to shout for his father, or the Asians might take fright; they seemed nervous as they stood dripping and shivering. What they needed was a hot drink, and he picked up the kettle.

He was taken aback by the change that came over them. Rows of white teeth and wide smiles. Their spokesman exclaimed, 'That is a kind thought, young sir,' and someone lit the gas stove. The tin of tea was discovered, and everyone became busy. Martin slipped from the room and up the stairs. His knock was not answered and he went in and shook his father's arm. The cold wet hand woke his father instantly.

'Smugglers!' Martin blurted out.

'Now look here –' his father began.

'Really, Dad. Not drugs. Men. They are in the kitchen. I'm afraid the other men will come after them.'

Though he did not fully understand, Mr Cornford knew Martin was serious and he pulled a sweater and trousers over his pyjamas. Mrs Cornford did the same, only asking, 'Where's Tim?'

'He is in the kitchen, Mum. They are all having tea. I hope you don't mind. They are so wet.'

The kitchen was full of steam and the noise of cups and chatter, but silence fell as the door opened. The Cornfords surveyed the scene for a moment. Then Mr Cornford said cheerfully, 'Good morning, all.' Even those who could not understand sensed his friendliness.

Their spokesman said, 'Oh sir, we are ashamed of the mess we are making in your beautiful house.'

Mrs Cornford went across to Tim. 'Fighting again?' she said. Tim managed a smile. 'Come along and I'll see if you need any stitches.'

Willing hands helped Tim to his feet, and he thanked them as, with his mother's help he limped from the room. As he left she called out, 'Get them something to eat, Martin; you know where everything is.'

While Martin got the food and had them all sitting at the table, he could hear his father on the phone; then Mr Cornford joined them in the kitchen. Martin left him with the men and went into the sitting room. Day had really come, though the rain blurred the distance. Something was moving on the farm road, it looked like a mini-bus. It turned in at the open gate of Mr Stevens' field. He watched as a couple of men got out, walked towards the sea and disappeared among the thorn trees.

He went back to the kitchen. His father strolled over to

him, stepping over the wet legs stretched out to an electric fire.

'They have come for them,' Martin muttered. His father had taken everything so calmly that he felt there was no need to explain.

'With blue lights?'

Martin shook his head. 'Not blue. A red mini-bus up in the field.'

'Oh, Mr Stevens will take care of that. Just nip upstairs and let me know which to expect first, field party or village.' He showed Martin the back door key. 'I've locked it, just in case.'

Martin went upstairs not quite sure what his father meant, except that he was to warn him before anyone came.

His mother called out, 'I'm putting Tim to bed. He's had quite a bang.'

Martin went into the bedroom and Tim asked, 'What's happened?'

'I've got to watch. They've come in a bus. I have to look the other way too. Something blue, Dad says.'

He walked across to the other bedroom. A mist shrouded the village, but he could see the road where it started its winding descent to the sea front. Nothing was moving. He went back to Tim's room, and from the window saw two men. They were coming down the field towards the cottage. He ran down the stairs.

He had just warned his father when there was a knock on the front door and at the same time someone banged at the back. Then a face looked in at the window and pandemonium broke out. Everyone seemed to be talking at once, mostly in a foreign language. Those in the kitchen were asking to be let out. Those outside demanding that the door be unlocked. Mr Cornford, meanwhile, was busy pretending that he did not understand what was being said.

40

It was obvious that the men outside were furious, and when one shouted that if the door was not opened at once someone would get hurt, Martin was afraid for his father's safety. What chance would he have if they attacked him? The Asians seemed more frightened than dangerous, but they could change. One of them was struggling to open the old-fashioned sliding window, and was getting angry.

At a signal from his father Martin ran back upstairs and found Tim out of bed, standing by the window. 'Look, Martin, look! Mr Stevens on his tractor.'

'Dad must have phoned –' Martin began, then stopped as a siren wailed. He crossed to the other room. From there he saw two police cars with blue lights winking from their roofs speeding down towards the village.

He lent over the banisters. 'They are coming, Dad. Blue lights.' Then he darted back to Tim who called excitedly, 'Look! Quick!'

The two men who had been banging on the doors had left the cottage and were on their way back to the mini-bus at the gate. They were finding it hard to walk fast on the slippery field.

'What will they do to Mr Stevens?' Tim cried. 'He has blocked the gate with his tractor and they'll never get the bus past it.'

Martin started for the door. He must help Mr Stevens if he could. Before he reached it Tim called out, 'It's all right,' and Martin saw two policemen rounding the cottage. They shouted to the men to stop, but instead they started running.

The policemen were young and very fast and in spite of the wet grass they overtook the men just as they reached the gate. Like shadows through the curtain of rain the boys saw Mr Stevens jump from his tractor and join them.

In the house all was silent and Martin thought of the

Asians standing helpless in their wet clothes. He slumped into a chair wondering what would happen to them now. 'I wish they *were* packets of drugs,' he said to himself, 'I wish we hadn't . . .'

His father called, and he got up and went slowly down the stairs.

The Broken Brooch

THERE was no one in sight. Justin had walked for two miles along the riverbank and had seen no one. The local policemen had the fishing rights of his father's farm and Justin enjoyed watching them and hearing their quiet talk as they relaxed on their days off. Sometimes he brought his own rod and joined them, but today he had been late home and knew that all he could hope for was to walk back to the road with them and hear what they had caught.

It had been hot in the crowded room where he had spent the afternoon. The special lesson had been interesting. It had been on the Roman roads of Sussex and the iron workers who had lived in the forest. The best moment came when a broken bronze brooch was handed round, for it had been found near the Roman road that crossed their farm.

It was a grey evening with a mist rising from the river and the damp water meadows. He wished he had pulled on a sweater, but it would be warmer if he went home by the footpath that led away from the river and joined the road back to the farm.

The footpath ran beside a fence. On one side the land rose to a low ridge. Here the grass was short, for sheep had lately been there. On the other side of the fence cows were grazing in a water meadow, half seen through the rising mist.

Justin had only walked a short distance along the path when he stopped. The shifting mist parted, and on a post ahead of him he saw a kestrel sitting, upright and still. They stared at each other for a few seconds; then the kestrel flew off above the low mist towards a distant

45

wood. Justin hoped he might see it again as the footpath
ran through the wood.

He started forward, then stopped again as a movement
caught his eye. Two men were crouching in a patch of tall
fern over which the kestrel had flown. For a moment he
thought they might be fishermen, but there was something
odd about them. Were they hiding? They were not hiding
from him, for he could see them quite plainly. They would
be hidden from anyone coming down the steep field, but the
field was empty. The mist was no more than knee high and
the broad road, with its stony surface, appeared and disappeared as the mist drifted over it. The road ran down the

hill, bordered by neat ditches. The fern, in its summer green, had been cut well back from the road; only at the bottom of the hill it had been overlooked and now filled part of one ditch. It was there that the two men were hiding. He wished that he had his dog with him. He would have barked at strangers and rushed to greet friends, and he had a feeling these were not friends.

The two men wore rough working clothes, but he was sure they were not locals. They were dirty, with long tangled hair and uncut beards. Then he remembered that his father had once had some sheep stolen. Were these men planning another raid? He found that, like the two men, he had crouched down, though there was only the thin mist which hid him at one moment and left him exposed the next.

Then he saw one of the men carefully part the bracken. As he leaned forward to see up the hill Justin noticed something in his hand that glinted. He, too, looked up and now saw a man at the top of the field where the road came over the brow. He walked down the road with quick decided steps. Justin let out a sigh of relief. Though he did not recognize the man, he would get up and walk with him till they were well clear of the two lurking men.

The man was wearing a kilt; breeches covered his knees; he had bare legs and sandals, and on his head a crash helmet. This seemed odd as Justin could not remember hearing a motor bike. He had a cloak thrown back over his shoulders and fastened under his chin. In his hand he carried a small bag. A rather strange outfit for a hiker; yet he looked a man to be trusted.

Something made Justin glance towards the two men in the bracken. They had half risen, like runners at the start of a race, waiting for the pistol shot. 'They are going to beat him up,' Justin thought. 'I must shout and warn him.'

By this time the walker had reached the bottom of the hill, and as he passed the two men Justin jumped up. At that moment they leapt from their hiding place. One swung a club which caught the unsuspecting victim on the back of his head and felled him. Before he hit the ground the other man lunged at him. One seized the bag. Plunging his hand into it he let a handful of coins run through his fingers; while the other man wrenched at the cloak till the fastening gave way; then with their spoil they ran off towards the wood.

The mist curled round the figure that lay stretched on the road. Justin could feel its cold breath as he stood stunned by the sudden tragedy. He wanted to turn and

48

run, afraid that the two men might look round and see him standing there; but they were by now only just visible. They ran towards the wood, their wild hair streaming above the mist as if a strong wind was blowing, though nothing stirred.

He looked towards the body lying so still. 'Perhaps they only knocked him out,' he thought. 'His helmet should have protected him.' He had to go and see, though his feet felt like lead. The silence was complete, as though he were shut in some cave far underground.

When at last he stood over the fallen man he saw with horror a crimson thread that crept among the stones. So the man had used a knife when he lunged forward. It must have been a vicious blow, for the man was wearing a thick leather waistcoat. He knelt down, wondering whether he should try and undo the leather buttons or run for help, or whether he should try and take off the helmet that was strapped under his chin. The outflung arm was warm and he felt for a pulse in the strong sunburnt wrist. He could feel no movement, but he was not sure if he had the right spot. He dragged out his handkerchief and tried to stop the flow of blood; but it was no use. He felt he was only wasting time.

'I must get help,' he thought.

As he backed away he caught sight of the buckle that had been wrenched so roughly from the cloak. It hung half hidden in the bracken. He felt sure he had seen it before. A broken brooch. The mist seemed to cloud his brain and he could not think where he had seen it. He reached out, but before he could pick it up a gust of wind shook the bracken and the brooch slipped between the fronds and vanished.

Fear returned. Fear that the murderers would come back and accuse him of stealing it. 'I must go,' he repeated. 'Not by the wood, they'll be waiting for me.'

He struggled to get up for the mist weighed him down.

Then he saw that he was too late. They were there already. Not the wild men, but men with bare legs and sandals like the murdered man. He twisted his head and found them all around him. He and the dead man in a circle of legs, walled in, with the mist slipping in and out between them.

He screamed, 'I didn't kill him!' and found he had made no sound. Perhaps it was the brooch they wanted, and he tried to tell them what happened, but the words would not come, and they stood there saying nothing. He took hold of the dead man's arm and shook it, hoping he might yet revive and save him.

A hand came groping out of the mist towards him, then a face appeared close to his own – a face harsh with anger and grief. Without a word the man bent lower till the cloak he wore fell forward over Justin's face, blotting out the light. In the darkness he struggled to free himself from the thick folds.

It was dark because in his fear he had shut his eyes. Now he opened them into a suffocating red mist. Gasping for breath he tried to push the cloak aside, but his hand closed on nothing. He could taste the wool where it pressed against his mouth, yet he could see through the cloak to a man standing behind. To his horror the man stepped forward and Justin looked right through him to yet another man standing behind, helmeted and with a short sword in his hand.

Suddenly Justin's mind cleared and he knew who they were, these men in their kilts and leather waistcoats. 'Romans! You are Roman soldiers!' he cried.

Now he saw that they were not looking at him, but at the dead man at his side. He sprang up and with all his strength flung himself at the enveloping cloak, plunged through it and through the two soldiers. Meeting no resistance he fell heavily.

His first thought was that his hands would be cut by the flinty road, but they were gripping tufts of grass, and he was stretched on the green hillside. The air was cool and fresh and the first star shone in a clear sky.

Slowly he turned his head. The mist was trailing up the hill. Were they carrying their dead comrade? Was it a cloak he could see disappearing over the hilltop? It was only mist, for there was no sound, nor was there a road for them to walk on; it was buried under the turf.

There was no body lying near by. Had the man been murdered for the money that he carried? Had it been to pay the iron workers? The remains of their workings lay in the field near the river.

Though his legs shook, Justin got up, 'They were ghosts, only ghosts,' he told himself, and yet the murdered man had seemed so real. His handkerchief lay a few paces off. He stood over it, then knelt and picked it up. There was no blood on it, it was just crumpled and rather grubby. It had been lying beside a shallow trench from which the turf had been rolled back, and the edge of the Roman road with its stony surface exposed. He stretched out his hand to the spot where he had seen the brooch fall through the bracken. There was no bracken now. The trench had been dug by an archaeologist and his team. So, the brooch he had held in his hand that afternoon, was the same one he had seen torn from the cloak.

'I could go home through the wood,' he thought. 'Those murderers have been dead nearly two thousand years.' But he decided that it would not take much longer if he went across the fields. He climbed a gate and started slowly till his legs stopped trembling.

Clash

I F you are wondering why I have a Danish wife and yet live in a Saxon village, I will tell you; only don't call Helga a Viking just because her hair is like spun gold.

Her father was a Viking all right, a real pirate. He and his boatload of relations attacked a village near us and slaughtered everyone who tried to defend his home. Our small village had not enough men to fight them. We had to submit right away, so they spared our lives; but they made us pay them a lot of money, and they drove off most of our sheep and cattle to stock their own farms. They settled on that hill over there, not a mile away.

I learnt all this later, being only a baby when it happened. I grew up hating and fearing the Danes for they often clashed with the men of our village. They were forever demanding payment from us, and thought nothing of killing a man if he refused to part with something they wanted. Yet they never harmed me as I roamed the woods searching for herbs and roots for my mother. She could cure most ills with the potions she made.

I met Helga by chance. The first I saw of her were her hands reaching up out of a bed of nettles. I stood and watched, wondering why anyone should choose such an unpleasant place to lie. Her hands gripped the trunk of a tree for a moment, then they slipped out of sight and I heard her groan.

I beat the nettles flat and found her with one foot twisted under a branch that had broken off the tree above her. Two or three pigeon's eggs lay near, so I knew what she had been doing. I got the branch from under her while she bit her lip till it bled, so I must have hurt her. I asked her why she hadn't shouted for help.

She tossed her hair back from her face and answered haughtily, 'We Danes don't cry for help.'

She was wrong about that as you shall hear; but at that time, though she needed help, she hadn't asked for it. When she did manage to get up she couldn't stand alone. One ankle was very swollen and she would have fallen if I hadn't steadied her. She couldn't put her foot to the ground, so in the end I had to carry her on my back, and that was not easy as she was as tall as me. I was frightened when I reached their farm gate, as I had often been warned not to go near; so I was surprised when the Danes thanked me in quite a friendly way for bringing Helga home, and told me I could come again.

After that we often met. I would stand just outside the farmstead and whistle a blackbird call, and if Helga was free she would pull back a thorn branch and squeeze through the hedge not bothering to go round to the gate. I would help her collect firewood, and she would show me where to find the plants that mother needed. Then we would go for miles exploring the forest, finding rare plants, discovering hidden ponds full of thatching reeds, or perhaps a nest of duck eggs. We might bring back a basket of nuts or blackberries, or anything that was of use. If her basket was heavy I would help her carry it into her home.

I loved her house. It wasn't like my home which was small and round with mud walls and a turf roof. The Danish house was like an upside down boat, thatched almost to the ground. Hanging from the beams inside were great iron shields with axes and spears stacked near them and helmets lying on the cross beams. Round the walls beds were fitted for all the household. You never saw so grand a home. Twenty at least were living there, while the horses and cattle were kept the other side of a partition.

Helga's father, Olaf, was taller than any man I have

seen and quicker tempered. He would snatch up his battle axe and swing it round his head while his blue eyes flashed fire and his yellow hair danced on his shoulders. Whoever had angered him would make off in a hurry, or he would never have a chance to hurry again. The great strength behind the sharp blade would have cut the man's head off at one blow.

One day Helga and I found some clay and sat in the doorway making pots. At least Helga was doing so; I was no good at it and mine fell to pieces. In the end I started tossing lumps of clay in the air. I don't know what got into me for I aimed a lump at Olaf's helmet. I shall never forget it. The helmet was on a beam just inside the doorway, lying on its side and the lump of clay went right in. The helmet rocked but didn't fall. I jumped up hoping to scrape it out, but the beam was out of my reach. Helga's eyes were wide with fright and I expect mine were too for at that moment Olaf came towards the house. I seized Helga's pigtails and at once we were on the ground fighting, hiding our fear. Olaf stepped over us as if we were not there. He never looked at his helmet, but I didn't dare go back there for days.

Some months later Egbert, the headman of our village came one night to see my father. Father could not go to the village meeting because a tree he had been felling had twisted in its fall and crushed his foot. Mother tried all her herbs and charms but it was months before he could walk, and he still limps.

They hadn't been talking long, before I felt a lump in my throat and, before I could stop them, tears were running down my face. I bit the rug that covered me so that no one would hear me crying like a baby. It was all so sudden and brutal. Egbert spoke as if it was just a plan to kill wild animals, though it was the Danes that were to be murdered while they slept.

My father spoke angrily saying that the Danes had been settled for years and were becoming good farmers. When Egbert told him it was an order from the king, my father was so rude about King Ethelred that Egbert got angry and said that father would be punished. To which he replied that as he couldn't walk it seemed that he would either be killed by order of the king or by the Vikings in revenge. Egbert didn't like the talk of revenge and tried to persuade father that there would be no Danes left to take revenge. All over England they were to be massacred that very night. Then he went away.

A sob burst from me. Father said angrily, 'Legs were made before tears.'

I threw off the rug and went to him. Crying had made my eyes feel as though nettles had stung them, and I could scarcely see, but I could tell by his voice that it wasn't with me he was angry. He spoke low and urgently. 'If you want to save her, don't just stand there. Get out.'

I didn't know he knew about Helga, for I had never told him, but there was no time to ask. In my hurry to go I stumbled over the calf lying asleep and catching the beam to steady myself, I knocked a hen off her perch. At any other time I would have laughed at the noise and confusion but this time I was out through the door and standing in the moonlight with no thought in my head except his words. The cold night air on my hot face suddenly made my jumbled thoughts quite clear. I don't know if legs were made before tears, but I knew what he meant and I started running.

My feet were cold on the frosty grass for I had forgotten to pull on my shoes; not that I minded for I went barefoot more often than not. It wasn't the cold that brought me to a stop, it was the sound that came from the low thatched houses round me. A harsh sound, and I shrank down in the shadows, for it came to me that if I were caught going to

the Danish farm that night, I could expect no mercy, young as I was.

The noise went on steadily, iron on stone; knives being sharpened for killing. I crept from shadow to shadow till I was through a hole in the village fence.

A newly ploughed field stretched ahead of me to the far woods, sparkling with frost in the moonlight. I leant back, afraid to leave the darkness. Then a murmur sounded behind me, warning me that the men were leaving their homes and I ran stumbling over the frozen ground. I felt sure I would be seen, yet I reached the safety of the trees and no one had shouted after me.

I thought my heart would burst through my ribs it pounded so hard as I raced up through the wood by the winding path I always took. I knew every inch of the way, yet the moonlight played tricks and I fell more than once. I reached the thorn hedge round the farm and, dragging aside the loose branch, I tumbled through, and started whistling my blackbird call.

It never struck me till afterwards that it would sound strange in the middle of the night, nor did I stop to think that Helga might be sleeping. I had scarcely begun when she was there, in the doorway, her face white in the moon-light. I ran to her not thinking what I should say. She stepped back into the house and I followed. What I saw froze the blood in my veins. I hadn't known that fear would be so cold.

The house was full of people and for a moment every eye looked at me, and there was no kindness anywhere, just a deadly quiet. The only sound was from the horses beyond the partition stamping and jingling their harness. One man had seized his throwing axe and it swung round his head in a slow circle. Even while I waited for it to leave his hand I saw the whole scene lit by flaring torches, the men arming themselves and the women packing things into bundles. The axe was never thrown for Olaf stepped up to me. I can still see the sharpness of his great battle axe. I was sure he was going to cut my head off but I forced myself to look up into his face. As I looked I could feel warmth coming back to me and with it the pain of a cut toe, and my cheek where a bramble had dragged across it.

Olaf looked over my head. When he saw that I was alone the cold fury left his face and he stared at me, faintly puzzled. 'Why have you come?' he asked.

'For Helga. She'll be safe with us,' I answered.

Then I saw that Helga was clinging to the doorpost, her face all streaked with tears. She cried out, 'I won't go with them. I don't want to go on the warpath.'

It was I who was puzzled till Olaf said, 'I thought the men of your village were close behind you, for we have been warned that the king has ordered the massacre of all Danish people tonight. We have no wish to fight your people who have been good neighbours, so we go to join our chieftain. If Danes are killed tonight then Saxons will be taught a lesson they won't easily forget.'

'I won't go!' Helga shouted again. 'I won't see the children killed.'

I was horrified to hear what she said, though I had often heard tales of Viking cruelty.

'You will stay in camp,' her father told her sternly. 'What happens is nothing to do with you.' She only sobbed louder.

He turned to me. 'This is your fault, teaching her soft ways, but we have no time to drag her along unwillingly.' He went on to tell me that if I took care of her, and they were not attacked as they left the homestead, then no one in the village would be harmed. As he finished speaking he reached for his helmet.

I expect the clay I had thrown in had been cleaned out, for Olaf often polished his war gear, but terror returned as I thought of the hard dry lump of clay falling on his head. I am ashamed to think that a thing like that should have added to my fears, but never play tricks on a Viking or you'll find your mouth feels withered and dry like eating an unripe blackberry. I caught Helga's hand and without a word we fled.

We hadn't gone far when Helga pulled me to a stop, and we stood holding our breath. The path through the woods at this spot was quite near the road that led up the hill from our village. From the road came the sound of men treading softly. Our sharp ears heard a twig snap and the sound of iron knocking on iron, followed by a muttered angry word. I knew I must stop them, or all the men from our village would be cut to pieces if the Danes were still in their homes.

Do you blame me that I hesitated? With Helga's hand in mine what would have happened if they had leapt the ditch and caught us? Would she be the first to die? Or would I die first, with no time to tell them that I had given no warning to the Danes that they were coming? As I stood undecided, their leader, Egbert I suppose, gave a shout. At once the whole silent band let out a yell. I expected them to rush forward, but I think no one wanted the honour of arriving first, and it took them several minutes to reach the thorn hedge round the homestead.

We stood listening to the shouts, waiting for the Danish battle cry. It never came. I could see Helga in a shaft of moonlight facing her home, waiting for the terrible moment when her father and all her family would fall on my Saxon friends and relations. As I watched, her face changed from moon white through pink till it glowed red as the thorn hedge was set on fire. As it blazed the sky became the colour of blood. Then with shouts dark figures ran leaping round that lovely house with its neat thatch and its arched doorway, and they flung flaming branches on to the roof till the air was filled with smoke and flying sparks that drifted down among the trees, setting fire to hollies and brambles. If it

had been summer time the whole wood might have burnt.

I could feel Helga trembling. 'They could all be dead,' she whispered. 'Father could have waited and killed them all.'

I knew this was true, and yet because of a promise not to harm our village if I took care of Helga, the Danes had left their home unguarded. She turned her back on the fiery remains of her home and faced her new life with her head held high.

The village men returned later singing a song of triumph, telling how the Danes ran away at the sight of them. They have never learnt that Helga watched them burn her home; yet when they boast of their brave deeds that night she can silence them with her look of scorn.

That is how Helga comes to be here, and why our house is long and not round. It is rough and poor as you can see and not at all like the fine house where she was born.

NOTE

It was Ethelred the Unready who ordered the massacre of the Danes on November 13, 1002, for he had been told they were planning to kill him. It is not recorded if any were slain, but the roving bands of Vikings and those Danes who had already settled, needed little excuse to continue their reign of terror in the towns and villages of eastern England.

The Black Bog

THE men of the village were sitting on the ground, their legs stretched out in front of them, their backs against a grassy mound. It was not easy to decide what to do, and they had made things no easier by sitting in a row instead of a circle; but they found it more comfortable to lean against the grave mound of their long dead chieftain while the north wind whistled over their heads and went singing and sighing through the rough grass that covered the smaller graves.

Witgar the tanner leaned forward. 'I say he has got to be stopped. Once he finds the way he will come back every year.'

'And take our pigs and cattle. We've no money for him!' Saxulf added. The others nodded gloomily.

That very morning a horn had sounded in the woods near the village and a man from Fletching had come bringing news. A monk from the Priory at Lewes, on his yearly visit to Fletching collecting the taxes, had asked about a village in the woods which had long been forgotten, and had demanded a guide. The Fletching men who were as afraid of angering the forest villagers as they were of the monk, tried to put him off. But he had insisted, saying he would be back in the morning when a guide must be ready.

Anlaf, the headman, looked up at a wooden cross on top of the grave mound. The monks had found their way to the village many years before, bringing Christianity to the village and taking away a tax for the Priory and the King. The monks had said they would come every year, but the villagers blocked the paths to their forest clearing and had not been troubled again.

They had never liked strangers and travellers coming their way had been known to disappear. The Fletching man had lost his way several times. He had kept blowing his horn to show he was friendly, and he was glad to find himself sitting among the graves with a mug of ale in his hand listening to the men as they planned how to stop the monk without blame falling on them.

Anlaf got up and faced the others. 'We'll ask them to guide the monk as far as the ferry –'

'That's not the best way!' Saxulf the smith broke in.

'Why should he come the easiest way?' Anlaf retorted. 'We don't want him here, and we don't want him to find the way another time. So – let him come by the ferry. Once he gets this side there's the path, and if he watches the way he should get here.'

'Which is just what we don't want,' grumbled Witgar.

The man from Fletching got up. 'We'll get him to the ferry,' he said. 'The rest is up to you.' He finished his ale and went back to his village.

Anlaf turned to Witgar. 'I said *if* he watches the way, but if we block the path where it leads up the hill, and if we do it cunningly, he'll follow the track round by the black bog and, with luck, get back to where he came from.'

Witgar grinned, 'Unless he falls in the bog.'

'He won't be the first to drown there, but the track does go round the bog. He's only to keep a sharp look out.'

So they planned it. They also decided to have two boys at the spot where the path was blocked in case the monk proved sharp-eyed.

'I'll send Alf,' Anlaf said. 'He could meet the monk and make him get on the track we want.'

'I'll let Edmund go too,' the swineherd called out. 'He and Alf should be able to manage him.'

As the men got up a large red face appeared over the top of the grave mound. It belonged to Rob, the village giant. Head and shoulders taller than anyone, and much stronger,

he felt he should be included in the village meetings, but he
lacked brains and was never asked to join. Now he shouted
after them, 'I heard! You aren't to do it. He'll fall in the
black bog and no one ever gets out once they fall in.'

The March morning was fine and the sun warm. Sheep like
flowers spread over the Downs, cattle
grass of the water meadows, smoke rose from farms and
birds sang. Brother John noticed none of these things as he
rode north from Lewes. Though he nodded a greeting to
those he passed, his thoughts were elsewhere. He was wondering why he had said he would find the lost village in
the forest and collect money from it.

The Priory was poor, yet the King kept demanding more
and more money. The Priory buildings were falling into

ruin so he had to find more money; but how much was he likely to get? The villagers would probably run away and hide when they heard him coming, and he might have to wait a long time before they came back. Then what if he lost his way; but there must be a road to the village. He had questioned a pedlar, but as he could give the village no name, the man had shrugged his shoulders and said he didn't know what village the monk was asking for, unless it was one on a bit of a hill beyond the river above some dangerous bogs. 'A rough place with rough people,' he had said.

The fields and the farms were behind him and the trees closed in as the road became a track; so little used that the branches brought down by the winter storms littered the way. So their progress was slow as the horse picked his way.

As he neared Fletching Brother John pulled his cow horn from his belt. The harsh notes echoed through the trees. Even though he had told them he was coming it was not safe to arrive without warning.

Having paid their tax, the people of Fletching did not run away when they heard the horn; even so Brother John was surprised they should greet him in such a friendly way. His horse was rubbed down, he was offered a pot of ale and a slice of eel pie, while a fresh horse was saddled for him.

It was pleasant sitting in the sun, and an hour slipped by before Brother John mounted the fresh horse and asked for a guide. A young man at once came forward and said he remembered the path and would put him on the way. They all shook their heads when he asked the name of the village.

'You are welcome to spend the night here on your way back,' someone called after him. 'We'll be on the watch for you.'

A woman lowering a bucket into a well spoke softly, 'No one can blame us if he comes to harm.'

The young man led the way on foot. The path twisted and turned. Brother John hoped he would remember the way. He had not thought there would be so many tracks and paths criss-crossing the forest. He made up his mind to keep the guide with him till he got back to Fletching.

The bright March day was changing. Dark clouds covered the sky and then the rain came, gently at first, pattering through the thin leaves. As it rained harder Brother John wrapped his cloak round him and pulled the hood well forward. The path became stony and ended at the river's edge.

'Blow your horn,' the young man told him. 'The river is too high for you to ford it.'

At the sound of the horn an old man hobbled out of a reed hut on the far side. Crippled with rheumatism like most of the older forest folk, he moved slowly. It took time for him to untie the rope that moored a raft; then with a long pole he brought the raft across the river.

The horse stubbornly refused to go on it though Brother John dismounted and led it forward.

The young man caught the bridle. 'Better leave him here,' he suggested. 'I'll tie him to this tree. He'll be all right till you get back.'

The last month had been very wet and the ground was waterlogged. Brother John was not going to walk. The day was dark under the heavy clouds and he wished he could turn back. He could tell them at the Priory that he had not been able to find the village, but he knew they would not believe him, and he would have to do the journey again. He glanced at the two men. The way they stood watching him made him angry. Were they trying to stop him? Had he really been shown the quickest way? Well! the nameless village was not going to escape as easily as that, so he said sharply, 'If the horse won't get on the raft he must swim.'

Seeing him determined, the two men pushed and pulled.

The horse suddenly decided to walk on to the raft and they crossed safely.

As Brother John remounted he looked round for his guide and saw that he was still on the other side. 'Go and get him,' he ordered the ferryman, but the young man called out –

'Len will show you the way. They don't like a lot of strangers, you'll be safer on your own.' And he turned away and disappeared in the rain.

Brother John looked down at the old man. 'How far to the village?' he asked.

'Not far,' Len replied. 'Just follow the path. If you're afraid to go alone I'll come with you.'

The idea that he might be afraid angered Brother John, just as the old man hoped it would, and he said, 'If my horse has to walk at your pace it will be dark before we get there. Put me on the road, and see that it's the right one.'

'There aren't any roads in the forest, but that path will take you there,' and Len pointed to a faint track that led from the river through tussocks of coarse grass to disappear among the trees.

The soft leather shoes of the forest people left only faint tracks behind them. As they walked they might cut back a few brambles, but if a tree blew down they would make a way round it, adding another twist to the already winding path. The winter rains made streams overflow and change their course. Old footbridges were often swept away to be replaced in a new spot. So the pathways changed from year to year. Only the locals knew where each one led as they took their pigs to the wallows or hunted for food. Towards this wild country Brother John now turned his horse.

'Is there just the one path?' he asked.

'One path that will take you there,' Len answered.

Brother John felt he was losing his temper and might say something that as a monk he would regret, so he dug his heels into his horse and splashed across the sodden ground towards the trees.

'Be sure and blow your horn,' Len shouted after him, 'or they might take you for an enemy.' Then the old ferryman went back to his hut chuckling to think he had frightened the monk.

The sound of the horn was deadened by the rain, but Alf and Edmund heard it, for it was the sound they had been listening for. Edmund was crouched by the holly bush that had been stuck carefully in the middle of the path. Though it was very prickly he crawled under it, holding on to the trunk in case the monk was not deceived and tried to push by. Alf picked up a bundle of firewood and started slowly along a track leading away from the village, hoping the monk would catch him up and ask the way.

Brother John drew rein beside the holly bush. Edmund held his breath afraid that the man had seen where the real path ran and was about to pull away the bush. No woodsman would have been taken in by a cut holly. He squinted up through the sharp leaves and saw the monk smile.

Brother John smiled because the sight of Alf walking ahead cheered him. A load of firewood being carried at the end of the day must mean that it was being taken home. He did not call out, not wanting the figure in front to run away. Hoping he had not been heard he waited a few moments and then followed.

On either side of the path the fading light was reflected in pools of water. His horse's hooves sank deep into the path which became narrower and narrower till the branches brushed his shoulders.

The young leaves were no protection from the steadily falling rain and he was soon soaked through. He did not see a low branch till too late, and though he ducked, a jagged piece caught in his hood jerking him off his horse. As he fell the cloth ripped and he was dropped among ancient brambles with great thorns that tore his legs and caught under the lacings of his shoes as he stumbled to get free.

His horse stopped and Brother John was able to grab the reins. The animal swung round and its hind legs slipped off the path down into the mud between the trees. Finding its legs trapped it threw up its head in fear, dragging Brother John back on to the path. Torn and muddy he struggled up speaking quietly to calm the frightened creature; then he tried to make it move, but it only snorted and rolled its eyes.

Thinking to catch the wood-carrier Brother John dodged under the horse's head. The path was still faintly visible and as he went along he blew on his cow's horn. Then he shouted, 'Hey! wait for me.'

He stood listening. The forest dripped and rustled. A few steps more and the path ended. Rubbing the rain from his eyes with a wet sleeve he peered about and saw that the track had not ended but had divided, turning sharply to left and right. Which way should he go? Suddenly a light shone between the trees to his left. Giving a shout, he hurried towards it.

Alf had not known what to do. He had thought the monk would catch him up and ask the way; then he would have pointed to the path that led back to Fletching, as his father had told him to. He was too shy to face a stranger and dared not go back to find out what had become of him. It had got so dark that he turned down a deer track, tossing his bundle of wood under a tree; then he stopped to light the lantern he carried for he was longing to get home, and even he could lose his way following deer trails in the dark.

As he picked up the lantern he heard the monk shout. So he had not gone home or taken the path to Fletching, but was coming after him. Alf lost his head. His lantern swung wildly for a moment, then he pulled his jerkin round it and plunged into the undergrowth.

Brother John reached the spot where he had seen the flickering light. There was no one there. Nothing but the trees outlined against the darkening sky, the tangled undergrowth, and a glint here and there of the water that lay stagnant in every hollow.

He was not easily frightened, but he had led a sheltered life among the monks of Lewes except for his tax-gathering trips, and then he was always on horseback. Now for the first time he knew what it was like to be alone in the wild forest where no one came and no one answered your call: the forest waiting, hostile, planning his death. No. Those were his own thoughts, he told himself angrily. A forest has no evil intention. A forest does not plan, and he had never believed the stories of the 'little people' with their lanterns who led travellers into bogs.

As he stood there under the dripping trees he wished he had not heard the story of the monster that had reared up from the mud with its thick body and long tail and its head high on a thin neck as it gazed haughtily round. As he looked this way and that it seemed as though the forest was full of moving shapes that hissed as they slid among the pools. He pulled his torn hood over his head to shut out the sound, but its sodden folds brought a silence that was worse than sound. He pushed it back and shouted, 'Where are you? I am a monk from Lewes. Show me a light.'

His cries did not echo among the trees, no breeze carried them through the rain; they died among the wet leaves at his feet. I will go back and get the horse moving, he thought.

As he turned he caught sight of someone standing in the path, he started running towards the figure. This time it was Edmund he saw. He had followed the monk and was standing where the paths divided; he hastily drew back as the monk ran towards him.

Brother John had poor eyesight and in the dim light he tripped over a root and fell, hitting his head. He struggled to his feet dazed and shaken, and ran on only to be tripped again. Once more there was no one in sight.

Now he felt sure he was being led astray. He had no idea which way to go, nor how to find the way back to his horse. Whoever had planned this confusion had been helped by the rain and the darkness; yet he must keep moving for the mist that rose from the ground was even colder than the rain that fell. He could tell he was still on a path, for though the ground was slippery and rough it was free of brambles.

Alf crept out of his hiding place and followed the monk till he met Edmund at the turn in the path.

'He went right by without seeing me,' Edmund whispered. 'Do you know he fell off his horse and left it stuck in the mud. I've started it back towards the ferry.'

'Listen to him,' Alf said. 'He's like a blind man. He could easily fall in the bog.'

Edmund turned away. 'He'll be all right if he goes slowly. It's a bit of luck he's chosen the Fletching path at last. Come on, I'm going home.'

Alf hesitated, then he said, 'I think I'll give him a light till he's past the black bog. It's got so dark.'

It was easy for Alf to get ahead of Brother John for he had blundered off the path and was standing helpless in the brambles with the rain dripping off his hair, down his neck and out at the ends of his sleeves.

Alf uncovered his lantern, but he did not answer when Brother John called out. He waited till the monk had regained the path then he went ahead, dodging about in case the monk tried to grab him.

Brother John followed the bobbing lantern. 'It's not an elf,' he said to himself. 'There aren't such things.' Yet he strained his eyes to see where to put his feet in case he was being led into danger. He thought of his brother monks back in the Priory eating their supper in the candle-lit hall. If he got back, he vowed he would never again venture beyond the Priory walls.

Someone was shouting in the forest behind him, and Brother John stopped. Alf looked back. He saw the monk standing with his arms outstretched as though he had been feeling his way. He knew who was shouting. It was Rob, the village giant, and he was calling, 'Where are you? Drowned! You're to be drowned!'

Alf was furious. He had done what he had been told, and had put the monk on to the right path. He was only doing a little more because the man seemed so blind; but what right had Rob to come interfering and trying to murder the stranger now he was headed safely away from the village. Forgetting his fear, he darted forward and caught the monk's hand, shining the lantern low so that he could see where to put his feet. Then he pulled him along.

Panic seized Brother John. He wanted to stop and pull himself together, but the terrifying yells behind him and the hand dragging him forward gave him no chance. The lantern at his feet helped him to see the way, though it was not bright enough for him to see clearly who held the light, only that he was not very big.

Rob had always been able to see better in the dark than most people, and Alf knew he would soon overtake them, so he pulled the monk to the side of the path and, pushing him behind a tree, he covered his lantern. Brother John was too bewildered to try and hide, he stood looking help-lessly back, his white face showing clearly against the dark tree trunk.

'Drowned! You're to be drowned!' shouted the great voice. A huge man sprang at Brother John, and a hand clamped round his arm in an iron grip.

Now there was no escape. He was rushed along and when he tripped he was swung back on to his feet with his arm half wrenched from its socket. The great creature kept leaning down and shouting in his ear, but his voice was too loud for Brother John to make out what he said. He could only guess that he was to be drowned without mercy and without time for a prayer. He cried, 'Stop! Stop!' but the giant paid no heed.

It did not cross Rob's mind that his captive could not see where he was going; that to him the forest seemed pitch dark. Nor did he think that the man he was dragging along was collapsing with exhaustion. It was a great tree lately fallen across the path that stopped him, and then only for an instant. He plunged off the path to get round it. Among the fallen roots were pools of water and Rob mistook a hole for a shadow and lost his footing. He let go his captive's arm and grabbed at a root to save himself.

The instant the grip on his arm was relaxed Brother John swung round and made off. Trees seemed to spring at him, and as he reeled back from colliding with one he was flung against another. His one thought was to find again the lantern that had shone at his feet and feel the guiding hand in his. Covered with bruises, his monk's habit hanging in tatters he still kept going, spurred on by the fear of the giant whose shouts he could still hear.

To his relief the trees thinned and the darkness paled and he came out into a clearing. He thought he saw a field stretching in front of him, and he paused, standing on a log that slowly sank under him. Then across the wide space in front, lights went bobbing. He called, 'Wait for me!' and started forward, thinking it was lantern light. It was not lantern light but the dreaded elfin lights that wandered over the black bog. His wild cry of horror as the mud rose round him was heard by Rob, and by Alf who came running to join him.

'Why? Why?' was all Alf could gasp out.

Rob's hands hung slack at his side. 'I don't know why.' He stamped his foot. 'I tell you I don't know. I was showing him the way and he ran off and wouldn't come back.'

'Of course he ran. You were going to drown him. You said so.'

'I never,' Rob exclaimed. 'I was taking him to Fletching, it was you who was leading him into the bog. I heard your dad say he would drown.'

'You great fool!' Alf cried, and darted off in the direction of the terrible cry, thinking of the awful day he had seen a piglet drown in the bottomless mud while he and Edmund tried in vain to save it.

Rob dashed off in the opposite direction, anxious to get back to the village and make out he had never left it, afraid of being blamed for the monk's death.

As Alf neared the bog the ground sank under him; mud slid over his feet and he caught hold of a branch to steady himself. A fallen tree, dead and rotten lay near, it bore his weight and he looked round for Rob to help him push it forward in the hope that the monk might reach it. Rob was not there and Alf could not move it alone. He inched forward and as he moved phosphorescent bubbles again ran like lantern lights over the black water of the bog as they rose from the rotting leaves and wood trapped deep in the mud.

Alf had shut his ears to the gurgling sounds that came from the bog, but suddenly he saw that the monk was not sinking but was swimming. The winter rain had filled the bog to overflowing.

For a moment Alf watched him in amazement. He knew the bog had spilled over into the forest, but he had never thought of the water being so deep. He whistled. It was not wise to shout for no one knew whether a monster still lived there. The black mud was seen to stir and bubble even on warm days, and some spoke of seeing a head thrust up through the slime. So he took no chances and whistled again.

This time Brother John heard, and stopped his frantic splashing as he churned up the mud searching for the bottom. 'Who's there?' he shouted.

'Hush,' came the answer.

Thinking the whistler was warning him about the terrifying giant, Brother John tried to keep his voice low, though fear made it hard for him not to cry out, and he called, 'Help me quick. I can't keep going.'

With no one to help him, Alf knew he had no chance from where he stood of getting the monk out of the bog. He shut his eyes trying to see the bog in summer time. There was just one place where some rocks overlooked the swamp, and it was possible from them to look down into the black water. If he could find these rocks in the dark there was a chance of reaching the drowning man from there.

The plight of the monk made Alf forget his fear of strangers and his fear of the monster, and he called out, 'Keep swimming. When I wave my lantern come to it.'

Then he dragged his feet from the mud and fought his way through the rotted trees round the edge of the bog.

He nearly gave up when he sank in up to his knees, and he wondered if it was worth while going on searching in the darkness. The monk could not possibly keep going for long in the cold and the mud, weighed down as he was by his heavy clothes. Suddenly there was firm ground under his feet, and he walked out on to a ledge of rock above the bog. At once he swung his lantern out over the swamp, calling 'This way! This way!'

There was no answer. The water lay black and silent. The thin rain that was falling left the surface unmoved. Away in the forest a wolf howled, and nearer at hand a frightened animal went crashing by. As Alf leant out over the bog the rushlight in his lantern flared and went out. In the darkness a thread of light crossed the bog. He shrank back knowing the danger, and one by one the bubbles burst and vanished.

It was cold standing there in his wet clothes, and though the rain dripped from every leaf and twig the forest was now wrapped in silence. He listened, feeling lonely and afraid – afraid that when he left the rock he might miss the path and there would be no one to come to his rescue; yet he must move.

He leapt back as the bog suddenly gulped as if it was swallowing. The mud stirred beside the rock and bubbles ran wildly over the surface. By their green glow Alf saw a black mass rear up and land on the edge of the rock. He was too terrified to move as it came sliding towards him, bringing with it the hateful smell of ancient mud. It grew tall and, in the darkness, seemed to tower over him; then it sank down with a moaning sound and Alf made out a man kneeling exhausted at his feet, while water and slime slithered off him. He heard a few muttered words, 'Save me – deep waters – over my soul.'

How the monk had managed to reach the rock Alf never

knew. As he stood looking down at the evil smelling figure he saw a hand, white against the rock, moving about as though searching for something. Crouching down he put his own hand on the rock and icy fingers crept over his, then closed round his wrist. Again he heard a whisper, 'Save me for thy —' The words broke off in a fit of coughing.

Alf straightened up. Brother John wanted to use both hands to heave himself up for his clothes were heavy, yet he dared not let go the thin wrist that was the only warm thing in a world of cold and fear. There was no lantern to guide him and he wondered in a dazed way if he had gone blind. He had struggled to get rid of his cloak as he floundered in the bog, but he could not untie the leather fastening. Now it weighed him down. Alf, for his part forgot his fear of losing his way. He thought only of getting the monk to Fletching before he died of cold.

Having lost one of his shoes Brother John hobbled along slowly and painfully. The bridge over the river had not been replaced and he had difficulty crossing on a fallen tree. His mind kept wandering. At times he thought he was riding his horse, while at others he imagined he was in the Priory chapel and would start singing, though the sound that came through his blue lips was little more than a sigh.

Alf's shyness returned as they neared Fletching, and he was afraid they might meet someone; but there was no one to be seen when the first cottage loomed up blacker against the dark sky.

Into Brother John's wandering mind came the fact that he was standing still. His way was blocked and his hand was on a latch. He rattled the latch and the door swung open. Warm air came to greet him and hands pulled him in. He looked with dull eyes at the burly man and his wife who drew him to their fireside. Neither of them owned the small hand he had been holding. He stared at his hand somehow expecting the other hand to be still in his.

'Where has he gone?' he asked.

'Gone!' the woman exclaimed. 'There was no one with you.'

Brother John shivered violently. The woman dipped a spoon into a pot simmering over the fire, while the man undid the leather ties of his cloak. 'The forest is dangerous at this time of year,' the man said. 'You were lucky to have found your way back here.'

'I was led,' Brother John insisted.

The man and his wife exchanged glances. 'Ah yes,' he said, 'but it's not always wise to follow their lanterns.'

Brother John slowly shook his head. 'Lanterns! Not safe! Giants – little people.' He swayed with exhaustion, and the man and his wife caught him before he fell.

The Reward

EDWIN stood listening. Then he bent down and went on hoeing the weeds that grew among the young bean plants; but he had not imagined the sound and he straightened up again. The strange throbbing sound was nearer and now he knew what it was – the thudding of horses galloping over the fields. Shouts and cries and the clash of weapons added to the noise. Edwin ran stumbling over the beans to the hedge. He pulled himself up on to the bank and peered through the leaves and gazed down the meadow in front of him. A little mist still hung over the river at the bottom of the meadow, but through it the sun struck flashes of light from weapons and armour. Horses and men struggled on the bank and as he watched, Edwin saw a man leap into the river followed by others, churning the quiet water to foam.

Edwin's attention switched to a group of men running towards him, the long grass catching at their feet, slowing them down. Knights on horseback detached themselves from the fighting by the river and rode after the running men who looked back at their pursuers. They must have known that they had no chance of reaching the hedge that might have given a little protection, for they stopped and faced the horsemen, shouting defiance, though many of them seemed to be unarmed. The knights rode towards them hallooing as if they were hunting wild animals. The soldiers were not animals, but young men from London eager to fight for freedom from oppressive laws. Yet they were rebels, for they fought against the king. Ill-armed and half-trained, part of de Montfort's army; they had attacked the town of Lewes only to be chased from the battlefield by the king's son, Prince Edward, and his knights, who showed no mercy in their fury at the Londoners' rebellion. For a moment the London men stood, bareheaded, in leather jerkins, facing the knights armed with lances, axes and swords. The next instant they were gone. Nothing showed in the long grass but an arm that seemed to wave farewell to the May morning before dropping back among the ox-eyed daisies and the trampled buttercups.

The knights drew rein, jostling round their leader. They did not pause long but came galloping straight towards Edwin. He had not noticed that on every side there were running men, and he thought the knights were after him. He leapt from the hedge and started running. The beans caught round his feet and tripped him. As he got up he saw other men crossing the field. Then the first horseman cleared the hedge and aimed a blow at the nearest man; but he dodged, and as the horseman went by he caught hold of the saddle and swung himself up behind the rider. Flinging his arms round the knight he drew a dagger from the horseman's belt. The blade rang as it slid across the helmet while the man tried to find a gap between the helmet and the chain mail. He had no time to get in a blow for another knight closed in with sword raised. The dagger flashed in the sunlight as it fell, and was followed by a lifeless body that slid over the horse's tail.

The knights crowded round. One shouted, 'Are you wounded, Prince?'

The knight pushed up his vizor and laughed, though it was not a pleasant sound. 'You gave him no time; but they'll pay for it. Come on.'

Edwin had been too frightened to move. He bowed as they streamed by, but they took no notice of the scared boy clutching his hoe. When they had gone he recovered enough to dart forward and pick up the fallen dagger. Hiding it under his tunic he ran across the field, through an open gate and down a lane to his home.

The farm labourer's cottage of daub and thatch gave little protection, and Edwin's father and mother had taken refuge behind it. It was lucky they had done so, for retreating soldiers had burst in and would have killed anyone trying to stop them from plundering. There was little enough left to steal, for the royalist soldiers from Lewes had driven off all the sheep and cattle to feed the army, but the Londoners took the little there was, including the crock of flour and the pot that had hung over the fire with a meal simmering in it. Only a few hours earlier the Londoners had marched by in silence to take up their positions on the Downs. Edwin had wanted to go with them to see the battle, but his father had held him back. How thankful he was not to be one of the fleeing rabble.

All was quiet so Edwin drew the dagger from under his tunic and held it out to his father, telling him how he had got it, and ending, 'The knights called him "Prince".'

'Prince!' his father exclaimed. 'Prince Edward! His dagger!'

The gold hilt with a jewel at the end caught the light. His father hid it under his coat looking nervously round.

'We'll be rich. You will be able to buy a farm of your own,' said Edwin, not understanding his father's fear.

'Rich!' His father thrust the dagger back into Edwin's hand. 'You put it back where you found it. It's not ours. Do you want to be hung as a thief?'

'The thought of tossing the beautiful dagger back among the beans did not seem a good idea. With everything stolen and the crops trampled, how were they to live? 'If I give it back to the prince,' Edwin said, 'he will give me a reward, won't he?'

His father still spoke angrily, 'Thieving or begging, I won't have it.'

'We could buy a new stew pot and –' Edwin's words trailed away as he remembered the speed with which the knights had ridden down the Londoners. He shuddered.

They had been given no time to speak. Would the prince think he had stolen the dagger and give him no time to explain?

His mother put her arm round him. 'The king will be in Lewes,' she said. 'He will protect honest folk, and the gallant young prince will be generous after his victory.'

His father snorted contemptuously, but his mother was already seeing visions of riches. 'A silver penny,' she murmured, 'new cloth for a skirt, and a cup –'

'Teaching our son to beg!' his father burst out.

His mother took no notice, though she now spoke softly in Edwin's ear. 'A reward is not begging. Just be respectful, and tell the prince how your poor mother has been robbed and how we will starve without –'

'That's enough!' his father broke in. 'Let him beg if he wants to. I'll never hear the end of it if I stop him.' He turned his back on them.

Edwin looked at the dagger. The point was turned where it had struck the armour, otherwise it was undamaged. He would never dare to try and sell it, but surely the prince would be pleased to have it back. Slipping it through the belt of his breeches and pulling his tunic down to hide it, he started off towards Lewes that lay about three miles away.

It would not have taken Edwin long to reach the town at any other time, but now the countryside was full of terrors. He nearly ran home again at the sight of a dozen or more Londoners hanging from an oak tree at the end of the lane. Not killed like soldiers but hanged like common criminals. There were wounded men begging for water or a hiding place. Peasants stripping the dead, ready to kill a rival. Grooms and pages searching for their lost knights or run-away horses. All these Edwin avoided, afraid they might ask what he carried.

He hid at the bottom of Offam hill as the prince and his knights rode back to Lewes on their sweating horses.

Bloodstained surcoats and crimson weapons decided him against trying to get through that great throng who thought they had won the battle. So it was past midday when he climbed the Downs by a sunken trackway. When he reached the brow of the hill that runs down to the walls of Lewes, he stood and stared. The wide hillside was covered with dead men. He went slowly down, picking his way among the bodies, around dead horses and over the litter of battle, broken swords, spiked maces, arrows that had missed their mark, spears and axes, lost shoes, torn coats and battered helmets. Above his head larks sang in the blue sky. Sounds of battle still came from the town. The dead lay so thick between him and the west gate that Edwin stopped. He could not believe that the tangled heaps in front of him had, only a few hours earlier, been hundreds of living men. He bent over a fallen soldier. Surely he was only resting, his blue eyes looked into the sky at something beyond Edwin's head. But there was no doubt he was dead.

A hand fell heavily on Edwin's shoulder. He cried out, thinking for a moment that after all the dead were really alive. His fears were hardly lessened by the look on the large bearded face that was thrust close to his own.

A rough voice spoke in his ear. 'Thought you would come thieving round the dead, did you? He was my friend. You keep your hands off him.' He held a knife under Edwin's nose. 'If you had been older you would have had this between your ribs. Get off home; we will strip our own dead and give them a Christian burial without help from outsiders.' He shook Edwin and let him go.

Edwin backed away, not noticing that his tunic had worked up and the dagger was plainly to be seen.

'Hey!' the man shouted, 'Give me that!'

Edwin did not stop to answer but turned and ran, jumping the fallen. He had not gone far before a spear rolled under his foot and he fell. The dagger was jerked from his

belt and lay shining in the sunlight. He put his hand over
the bright hilt and getting up, he looked behind him. The
man had not followed and was bending over his friend; but
there was a young soldier near by collecting fallen weapons.
Edwin slid the dagger under his tunic, hoping it had not
been seen. He went on his way, walking carefully, making
for the north entrance to the town where the Londoners
had hoped to break in, but from where the prince and his
knights had charged, cutting them down, before they broke
and fled. The chalk road that led to the town had been
ground to a white powder that covered the sprawled
bodies of the Londoners who had led the charge.

Edwin glanced behind him and saw to his dismay that
the soldier was following. He wore a steel cap, and on his
leather jerkin a white cross had been roughly stitched, a
sign that he was one of Simon de Montfort's men. This
meant nothing to Edwin; his only thought was to escape
the soldier, who carried a spear in his hand and shouted
'Stop!'

Outside the north wall of the town many poor people had
built houses. Shabby and badly built they leaned at all
angles over muddy lanes. Into this jumble of mean streets
Edwin plunged, turning first one way then another. An
alleyway with slime-covered stones slowed him, and before

he could reach another corner he heard again 'Stop! Or I'll kill you.'

There was a narrow turning just ahead of him and he made a dash for it, but the flung spear hit the side of his head, and carried away the top of his ear. He fell, hitting his head on the corner of a house. Half stunned he waited for the next blow to strike between his shoulder-blades; but he never thought of dropping the dagger. Conscious of a noise behind him, he flattened himself against the wall and looked back. The alley was blocked by two men. Their swords clashed and rang as they fought together. One was retreating, striving to keep his balance on the uneven slippery stones as he was pressed back. The young soldier who had been following Edwin, had been forced to squeeze into a doorway to avoid the swinging blades. He now held a sword in his hand, but the fighting men blocked his way.

Edwin could feel the blood running down the side of his face and his head swam, but he steadied himself and then dodged round the corner. The lane ran steeply up hill and at the top he could see the town wall. He sobbed with relief for he had heard that a path ran all round the outside of the wall. Perhaps he could confuse his enemy if he reached it before he came in sight.

He gained the wall safely, but the end house on each side of the lane had been built against the wall, defying the orders of the town Council. He beat on the nearest door but no one answered. In panic he searched for the latch and found only a piece of rotted twine which broke as he pulled it. He put his shoulder to the door, and with a shriek of protest it burst open and he fell into a room that smelled of dirt and damp. A little light filtered down from an opening against which a ladder was propped, and Edwin scrambled up it, pausing at the top to listen.

From the lane outside he heard footsteps, and by the way they stopped and then came nearer he guessed the soldier was searching the dark corners for him. A few more

steps and he would find the open door. Edwin kicked the ladder and heard the splintering of wood as it hit the floor. He backed away from the opening and found he was in a low attic. There was nothing in it but a pile of rags. It had no door and only a small shuttered window covered with cobwebs. Holes had been bored in the wood, letting in some light, but he could not find the catch to open the shutter.

From behind him came a rustling sound and he spun round. He could hear someone in the room below but the attic was empty. Then he saw the pile of rags moving, and he made out two red-rimmed eyes sunk deep in the withered face of an old man watching him. There came a thin whining sound as if the old man was trying to say something. Without a thought as to how the old man came to be there all alone, Edwin demanded, 'Where is the catch? I can't open the shutter.'

'Don't dare –' the old man began, then started coughing.

At the same moment the soldier called, 'Throw down that dagger or I'll come up and get you,' and the top of the ladder appeared through the opening.

Whether the ladder had not broken as it fell, or whether the soldier was bluffing, Edwin did not stop to find out. Perhaps the shutter was as rotten as the door had been. He threw his weight against it and with a crash it fell outwards nearly carrying him with it.

Instead of being against the town wall, there was a small yard below him. The wall was several feet away, the top a little higher than the window, but without caring what became of him he crouched on the window ledge and flung himself at the wall. His fingers gripped the rough stones. His legs thrashed wildly. Then one toe found a crack in the wall. He got a knee on to the top, rolled over and fell, landing with a thump that winded him. Then he rolled farther through nettles into a ditch where he lay trembling and faint, waiting for his enemy to land on top of him.

When nothing happened he grew calmer and he wondered if the soldier would really have killed him for the sake of the dagger. He peered down at it. Gold! though he had never seen gold before he could feel its power and knew its worth. The pure untarnished gold was twined like a snake round the hilt, holding the ruby in its setting. Only a prince could wear anything so beautiful.

He struggled to his feet and climbed out from the mud and rubbish of the ditch. He found a path leading up hill that turned into a street with houses, and he looked for someone to tell him where to go.

Two monks in black habits hurried by carrying a wounded soldier. 'Where can I find the prince?' Edwin asked.

They didn't stop or answer, but hurried on, while behind them smoke came curling up the street. A blazing arrow flew over Edwin's head, landed on a thatched roof and at once flames shot into the air. In the castle high above him, the royalist defenders were still holding out and were doing their best to set the town on fire, adding to the terror and confusion of the inhabitants. Everywhere he turned the streets were thronged; women ran calling for their children, lost children screamed. Old people were jostled as they wandered about. Thieves and pick-pockets dodged in and out of the crowds. A blind beggar went tapping by, crying for someone to lead him to safety. Soldiers shouted as they hunted the enemy and prisoners pleaded for their lives, and everywhere, under the hurrying feet lay the crumpled bodies of those who had not escaped.

Edwin leant against a wall not knowing what to do. A woman came by, and seeing his blood-spattered face she stopped. 'Get out of sight,' she said. 'They are on the rampage and will kill you.'

'I must find Prince Edward and give –' he began.

'Don't you know, the prince and the king have been

captured. They are in the Priory down there,' and she pointed down the street before hurrying on her way.

The street ended in a small postern gate through which came a cool breeze bringing a faint smell of the sea. Beyond the gate lay the Priory of St Pancras. There had been hard fighting between its walls and those of the town, and the dead were being collected for burial. A cart full of wounded creaked by, making for the gate of the Priory. By the gate soldiers with white crosses stood on guard. They let the monks go through with the wounded and, by keeping close beside a cart, Edwin got in without being stopped.

He stood by the Priory church where the wounded were carried in and laid on the floor. A monk standing near caught Edwin by the shoulder and looked at his ear. 'Painful but not serious,' he said. Edwin nodded; then wished he had not done so for it made him feel dizzy and his head throbbed. But he thanked the monk and then felt bold enough to ask if he knew where the prince could be found.

'That is easily answered. He is over there in our refectory.' Then the monk turned away to attend to the wounded once more.

Edwin followed a grey friar into the great dining hall. It was full of knights; their loud voices deafened him and he shrank against the wall.

When no one took any notice of him he looked about him. Long trestle tables, loaded with food flanked the walls. Some knights were eating, some sat too tired to move, while others strode about the hall.

Between the moving knights Edwin caught sight of a man sitting in a splendid chair. He had a purple bruise on the side of his face and he looked exhausted. Grey and black monks hung over him, bringing him messages or taking them away. Everyone bowed low to him, and Edwin guessed it was the king.

It was not hard to recognize the prince. A head taller than the rest, with a thatch of fair hair, his handsome face red and angry and his voice raised above the others, he seemed to be excusing himself for some fault. Suddenly he threw himself down on a bench and poured wine into a cup.

Edwin squeezed between two knights and found himself standing beside the prince. In the fields that morning it had seemed right that the prince should ride down the soldiers who opposed him; but why had he turned hangman? Had the terrified prisoners begged for mercy before he hung them from the oak tree? Should he beg the prince for a reward? He found that he couldn't do it and, without a word, he drew out the dagger. Holding it carefully by the blade he offered it to the prince. Prince Edward paused for a moment in the story he was telling and took the proffered dagger, holding it a moment as though expecting Edwin to speak; when he only bowed the prince thrust it into his belt and went on with his story. A knight pushed Edwin aside and he stumbled back.

'If you were expecting a reward you should have gone to Simon de Montfort at the Grey Friars. Victors are usually more generous than the defeated.' Edwin turned and found a tall monk smiling at him.

'I don't understand,' Edwin answered. 'The Prince won the battle. I saw him.'

'I am sure he killed a lot of men, but he was away too long. When he came back the king was already a prisoner.'

'The king is wounded. Why doesn't he rest?'

'De Montfort's barons battered him with their maces, and I heard he had two horses killed under him; but this is no time for rest if his kingdom is to be saved and his friends kept from ruin.' Edwin did not know the reasons for the civil war; it just seemed wrong that the king of England should be so ill-treated.

'Don't stand staring. Have something to eat,' the monk

told him, and pushed a cup of wine and a hunk of bread and meat along the table.

It was a better meal than any Edwin had eaten, but he had no time to linger over it for the monk beckoned to him from the doorway and they went out together. Before he understood where the monk was leading him, Edwin found himself among the cooks behind the great hall.

In front of him loaves of bread were piled on a trestle table, a knife was thrust into his hand and someone shouted 'Hurry, Hurry!' He cut thick slices of bread for hours till he was ordered away to pluck chickens and thread them on to spits. Then he had to carry cooked meats and cheeses to knights, pages and soldiers who lay on the grass or sat propped against trees, uncertain of their fate but ravenously hungry after the day's fighting. Edwin ran from one job to another, cuffed and shouted at while his head ached and his ear burned.

At last the sun set and as the sky grew dark he managed to slip unseen beyond the light of the blazing fires and out, unnoticed, through the priory gate.

Afraid to cross the battlefield in the dark with its litter of weapons to cut his feet and thieves to cut his throat, he crept round the hillside in the shadow of a belt of trees. The moon rising over the Downs struck a spark from something in the grass beyond the trees. Edwin shrank back. Before he had made up his mind whether or not to run away, a man in chain mail raised himself on his arms and called, 'Cuth.'

He was a royalist soldier, for Edwin could see that he wore no white cross. Wounded in the battle he had dragged himself away till his strength failed. Now he lay at the edge of the wood where it might be days before he was found.

Almost against his will Edwin stepped forward. 'I'm not Cuth,' he said.

The wounded man looked up at the boy in his rough clothes. In spite of his pain he spoke with authority.

'Catch my horse,' he said. 'He keeps moving away before I can reach him.'

Edwin found the horse under the trees. It had a leg entangled in the reins and was not hard to catch. It was much harder getting the wounded man into the saddle.

The horse took a step forward and the soldier swayed. 'Can you get home alone?' Edwin asked.

'Only five miles. He'll get me there.' He clutched the horse's mane with one hand, then fumbled at his belt with the other. 'No ransome. No ruin,' he mumbled as he took a coin from his purse.

Edwin's hands hung down. 'No,' he said. 'No reward.'

The wounded man's breath came like a sob. 'Was for Cuthbert. Soldier's pay. You've earned it.' He rode slowly away.

The silver penny in Edwin's hand shone in the moonlight.

HISTORICAL NOTE ON THE BATTLE OF LEWES

The battle of Lewes was fought on the 14th of May 1264. King Henry III and his son Prince Edward led the royalist army. Simon de Montfort led the army of the Barons. These wanted the government of England reformed, for the king had nearly ruined the country; but tne king wanted to keep all power in his own hands. So it came to civil war, and the two armies raged up and down the land till the king's army reached the south coast hoping to capture the ports. They were strongly defended and he was not able to do so. His army was tired, and so he brought them to Lewes, which was near by and friendly. It was a small town surrounded by thick walls and having a fine castle which stood (and still stands) on a high mound above the Sussex Ouse in a gap in the Downs. Here the king must have felt safe.

Simon de Montfort brought his army from London, spending one night camped in the small village of Fletching. Very early in the morning of May 14th he marched towards Lewes and climbed the Downs north of the town. He did not wait in the usual way for the king to bring his army out of the town and form up in battle array, but attacked down hill while the royalists were forming up.

With de Montfort was a large force of foot soldiers from London, poorly armed and ill-trained. These were ordered to attack towards the castle, but before they reached it Prince Edward led a cavalry charge against them. The Londoners turned and fled. The horsemen followed, killing all they could find. (A hill three miles from Lewes is still called 'Dead-man-tree'.) Meanwhile the rest of de Montfort's army had defeated the king's army, and when the prince returned to the town he was forced to join the king as a captive.

A number of pits full of bones have been dug up round the town, and it is reckoned that about five thousand soldiers were killed in the battle. Only a few knights lost their lives as they were protected by their armour. They wore chain mail covered with a sleeveless linen coat. Many had chain hoods, though some had helmets. The horses however had no protective armour, and many were cut down.

Shipwreck

JIM woke. He clutched the bedclothes up to his chin and lay listening. His bed trembled as the gale battered the house but that had not woken him, nor was it the noise of the storm or the distant roar of the waves pounding the shore. It came again, the sound that had woken him, deep and insistent, the boom of the lifeboat gun.

He jumped out of bed, groped for the door and flung it open. A light showed under the door opposite and he crossed the landing and burst in. The candle by his parents' bed was caught by the draught and went out. A match scraped and his father's shadow sprang up the wall, his head looking like a bird with a large beak; but the beak was only the Sou'wester that his father had pulled on and was now tying under his chin.

'You are dressed already!' Jim could never understand how his father got into his oilskins so fast, for he never seemed to hurry. 'I won't be a moment father. Wait for me,' he begged.

'No Jim.' His mother was sitting up in bed. She spoke firmly. 'No, it's dark. We would only get in the way.'

The shadow on the wall nodded, and Jim felt his father's hand ruffling his hair. Then he was gone. Even the sound of his boots on the stairs was lost in the rattle of the windows and the banging of his bedroom door.

It was hard to go back to his room and know he must miss seeing the lifeboat launched. Seeing his father and the other men high above him, their oars ready; while below men pushed the boat from its shed, starting it down the slipway till it met the waves and in a smother of foam the oars would rise and fall and the dangerous moment be passed.

A new lifeboat was due any day. A powered boat with an engine to do the work of oars. It would be launched from its own pier beyond the breaking waves.

Jim had told his father that he hoped the new boat would not come, for it would make the launching dull. His father had made no reply.

Jim dressed quickly, and he and his mother met in the kitchen where the steady flame of the oil lamp made the room seem calm after the wild shadows thrown by his candle.

'There is no need to gobble your breakfast, Jim. It will be too dark for an hour yet.'

Jim glanced up at his mother. He was not taken in by her quiet way of talking. He knew she was afraid. He wondered if she would be afraid when he joined the lifeboat crew.

She had no need to be, for they had both seen the lifeboat launched in stormy weather and return safely many times.

'I wonder what boat is in distress and where it is,' he said.

'The wind is from the east.' His mother looked at the barometer. 'I've never seen the glass so low. Lord have mercy on those at sea!'

Jim thought of the jagged remains stuck fast below Culver cliff, and the rusty iron in White Cliff bay among the seaweed covered rocks. They had been there all his life and were the remains of ships that had run for shelter and been caught by a wind and tide too strong for them. This might be yet another. He must get down to the lifeboat station. As he had not seen the launching, he must see the return. He peered through the window. There was a greyness in the sky behind the racing storm clouds.

'Let's go,' he said.

His mother was packing a basket; tea, sugar, milk; cups folded in a cloth. Then she buttoned up her coat and turned out the lamp.

. . . . .

Old men in oilskins, wet with spray, were on the slipway watching the great waves come rolling in. Too old to pull an oar they waited, hoping for a chance to lend a hand.

Jim tugged at a wet sleeve. 'Mr Bevis!' he called.

The old boatman looked down at him, then walked to the lee of the lifeboat house where they were out of the wind. 'You won't see nothing from here,' the old man said. 'She is stuck fast beyond the foreland. They are taking the rocket up there now. Drat my rheumatics.'

'I'll go and see what is happening.' Jim felt his mother's hand on his arm. 'I'll be all right. I won't go near the edge,' he assured her.

'There is quite a crowd up there already,' old Bevis told her. So she let him go.

As he left the shelter of the boathouse the wind caught and held him. He had to bend double, butting through the

wind as he started up the long slope to the foreland from
where he would see into White Cliff bay.

Before he was half-way he had to drop on to his knees
and turn his face from the wind, to get his breath. Then he

glanced seaward to see if the wreck was in sight, and his mouth opened and the wind drove back his cry. He clutched the turf choking and breathless for he had caught a glimpse of the lifeboat among the waves.

As he watched he saw it rear up from a deep trough, climbing so steeply he was sure it must turn over, but it perched for an instant on the top before plunging down the far side. The waves surged past and over the boat and the men strained at the oars, yet Jim could see that they were making no progress. Not all their strength was enough to drive the boat round the foreland in the teeth of such a gale. In sudden panic, he thought that if they tired, they too might be swept on to the rocks.

He would have stayed where he was on the soaking grass if some boys from the village had not come by and swept him along with them. As they went through a little wood of stunted thorn trees they shouted to him not to worry. Beyond the trees they met the full force of the gale. A group of people was standing bunched together all leaning forward as if the wind was a solid wall.

Jim screwed up his eyes against the salt spray that whirled over the cliff edge, stinging his face. Through the spray he could see a small ship wedged on the hidden rocks. Though lashed by the storm it still held together, still looked like a ship with a funnel and wheelhouse, only its angle was wrong. It was tilted sideways, with the remains of a boat dangling from its side.

Suddenly a wave sprang up beyond the stern, towered over the ship, broke and smothered her. A dark object was swept over the bows and hurled towards the shore.

The crowd made a queer gasping noise, then everyone was running in an odd slow way, pushing at the wind, forcing a way through. They went down the steps by the coastguard cottages and stumbled through the stones, hurrying along the beach. A wave crashed on the shingle and foamed towards them. They clung to the slippery lumps of chalk at the base of the cliff as icy water drenched them and filled their shoes; then it ran back dragging stones and seaweed with it. Jim grasped a hand and found himself part of a human chain with the leaders wading into the sea trying to reach the dark form that was carried towards them and then swept back from their outstretched hands. At last a limp body was brought ashore and carried up the beach. Jim struggled back through the shifting stones to the wooden steps.

Out on the reef the ship listed still farther and now Jim could see a group of men in the bows holding on grimly as the waves pounded over them, while up by the wheelhouse another sailor appeared, turning his head as though searching for a way to reach his companions. Then another great wave rolled over the ship and thundered towards the shore. The crowd came pushing by him up the steps bearing the drowned man in a rug, and when Jim looked again towards the ship he saw that half the wheelhouse had been torn away. From a broken railing there seemed to be a spider hanging from its thread, but he knew it was the pressures. Drift and thrust. Yes, thank ye, I'll have a cup of tea.'

Talk and argument and the rattle of tea-cups. Jim stepped back into a dark corner. With cold hands he felt for the muscles in his arms. Through his sodden coat he could feel how thin he was. Even if he grew to be as strong as his father he could still be too late – too late to reach a drowning seaman. Then he remembered the new lifeboat. A powered boat whose engines would drive her through the fiercest gale. 'Perhaps I won't have to wait till I am as strong as father,' he thought. 'With the new boat we should get there in time to save them all.'

sailor he had seen. As another wave curled over the ship he shouted 'Hold on!' though no one could have heard his shout. The wave must have lifted the man upwards for now he was stretched flat against the rails with nothing below him but the cruel sea. Jim suddenly understood that it was for this that his mother had been afraid, for an unknown seaman in peril. Soaked to the skin and shaking with cold Jim clung to the steps, waiting for the lifeboat that never came.

A gun cracked above his head and a line flew through the air and fell across the bows of the wreck. It was the rocket old Bevis had spoken of. Now the sailors could be hauled to safety. Would it save the man on the rail? A shaft of sunlight cut through the black clouds and for a moment the broken rails gleamed white; then they were hidden under a curtain of falling water, but not before Jim had seen that the sailor was no longer there. He stumbled up the steps. At the top he looked back once more, but nowhere among the breakers could he see a dark form; no swimmer appeared among the wreckage. Jim put his hands over his ears to shut out the sound of the waves and the mocking wind, and turning his back to them he ran.

The lifeboat was on the slipway and the men were inside the boathouse when Jim got back. The words he was going to shout at them slipped from his mind for in a shocked moment he thought they were all dead. Utterly exhausted they sat unmoving; only his father raised an eyebrow and Jim answered his unspoken question.

'They've got a line across the bows,' he said. 'They got it there at the first try.'

A man slumped in a chair got to his feet, and life seemed to flow back into all of them as they turned towards him. 'First try did you say?' When Jim nodded the man went on, 'Who said George was no good? Him and his wind